BECKONING
SHADOWS

. . . .

THE 3RD BOOK OF THE
ARKANSAS OIL DAYS SERIES

BRENDA HUTCHESON FICKEY

Beckoning Shadows

by Brenda Hutcheson Fickey

Trade paperback ISBN: 978-1-943294-02-2
Ebook ISBN: 978-1-943294-03-9

Cover design by Martijn van Tilborgh

Beckoning Shadows is also available on Amazon Kindle, Barnes & Noble Nook and Apple iBooks.

For more information and to purchase more books by Brenda Fickey, visit *BrendaFickey.com*.

CONTENTS

FOR

Traci, Brent, Kyle, Keremy, Olivia, Jason, Elizabeth, Michael, Joshua, Emma, Matthew, and William

DEDICATED TO

my dad and mom and the memories of Rosie (his mother), Joe (her first husband), Uncle CK, Uncle Arthur, Uncle Joe, Uncle Harold, Charlie (her second husband), and Aunt Mary

ACKNOWLEDGMENTS

THIS THIRD BOOK WOULD NOT have been possible without the help of some very special people in my life. First, I want to thank Kudu Publishing, Martijn, and the staff who work with me specifically. Thank you for believing in my stories and making them available to my fans. Without you, my career would be an unfulfilled dream.

Second, I want to thank several people in Smackover, Arkansas. The staff at the Arkansas Museum of Natural Resources graciously makes their archives and oral history libraries available to me. My research there continues to help me keep the setting true to the time and location for my Arkansas Oil Days Series. Thank you, Belinda, for your invaluable advice and help with transcripts. I also want to thank the staffs at the Smackover Public Library and the *Smackover Journal* newspaper for helping me with documentation about events I include in my stories. I also want to thank those in Smackover who stop me on the streets, in stores, in restaurants, and other places to share their memories. I enjoy the conversations and cherish the opportunities to keep this town on the map for a long time to come.

Third, I'd like to thank my family. Mom and Dad, you keep me wanting to tell these stories. I love how you watch the Smackover newspaper for valuable articles for my files. Thank you for answering my questions, no matter how silly they may sound, and for believing in me and what I am doing. Thank you, Olivia, Jason, and kids, for letting me set up my office in your home. Thank you, Traci, Brent, and kids, for encouraging me to keep on doing what I love. Thank you, Joni and Kay, for being part of my team to get this book written. Thank you, Olivia and Joni, for being my editing team. Your work challenges me to do my best, from the first draft through all the rewrites. It helps when your tastes in reading material match mine. You make sure my standard for high quality, if not perfection, is attained.

Thank you, David, for sitting with me to discuss the grieving process. Even though I am going through my own, you gave me insight for what a young man like Hank would experience in his grief. Thank you for allowing me to model my circuit preacher after you. I hope you see yourself in the character and are pleased with the results.

I also want to thank my test readers for their input and encouragement, especially with the turns the story took apart from my initial outline: Alex, Andrew, Angelica, Billie, Chris, Ginni, Hailee, Richard, and Sharon. Your help keeps me focused on the audience I want to reach. Thank you for helping me to tell a stronger story.

Fourth, I want to thank my readers. Without you, there would be no story to tell. I would love to hear from you about your experiences with the Arkansas Oil Days Series. You can email me at *whisperingdarkness@earthlink.net*. I also invite you to visit my website at *www.brendafickey.com* for information about all my books and future projects.

Last, I thank God for the guidance to follow His plan to write these stories. To Him be the glory!

CHAPTER 1

THE BACK OF HANK'S NECK tingled. He stared at the woods across the Ouachita River between Spoon Bend and Frenchport, unaware of anything else around him.

"Whoa, Hank! What are you doing?" Beth Ann grabbed his pole as he rubbed the spot on the back of his neck, just beneath his hairline.

"You're letting him get away. Are you crazy?" Daniel joined Beth Ann. Hank felt several strong jerks loosen his grip slightly.

"Come on, Hank, don't let him go." He saw Abraham look at something over the edge of the rock where they fished, barely conscious of the words being said. "Would you look at that? Help him pull. The tip of his pole is almost in the water."

With white knuckles, Hank grabbed his pole with both hands again. "Did you see that?" Everything moved in slow motion. Without warning the pole whacked him in the middle of his forehead. Falling backwards, he heard distant screams and yells and then he landed on something hard.

"His eyes are opening." Hank heard a girl's voice as though it was coming from the other side of a thick, black curtain.

Beth Ann? What happened? Hank raised himself up on both elbows, shaking the fog from his head. He tried to sit up, but several hands on his chest kept him down. *Where am I?* Feeling the rock's surface beneath him, his memory returned in a flash.

"Sit up slowly, Hank. I need to check for a bump." Beth Ann used gentle fingers to feel the back of his head.

"Aah."

"Sorry. It's not bleeding, but you do have a big knot."

"Check out the one on his forehead." Daniel's wrinkled brows told Hank it was big, too.

"What happened?" The world slowly spun when he stood and then his knees buckled.

"Not so fast, Hank. Help me, guys. He's going to faint." They all helped Hank lie back down.

"Wow, look how pale he is." The whites of Abraham's eyes glowed against his dark skin.

"He looks a little green, too."

"Be quiet, Daniel. You and Abraham help me get him on his side in case he throws up."

"I'm all right. I don't feel sick, really."

"You need to be still. You took quite a whack to your forehead with your fishing pole before you hit the back of your head on the rock. You might have a concussion. Look at me. How many fingers am I holding up?"

Hank pushed her hand away and put his fists at his temples, wincing. His head pounded with every heartbeat.

"If you think you're going to throw up, tell me."

Hank sat up slowly. Then he pulled one knee up to anchor his elbow as he rested his head in his palm.

"I don't feel like throwing up, okay? What happened, anyway?"

"You let old Methuselah get away." Daniel motioned for Abraham to help him get Hank on his feet.

"What did you see, Hank?" Abraham's voice sounded fearful.

"Huh? What did I see?"

"Yeah, you were saying, 'Did you see that?' just before your pole hit you." Daniel gradually released his grip.

Hank was steadier and felt stronger. He thought for several seconds, his brows furrowed. He looked around, at the rock where they fished from; Catfish Haven, their secret fishing hole; the Ouachita River just beyond that; and then the woods around them and across the river. His eyes were drawn to the treeline along the riverbank across from where they stood.

"I saw something over there." He pointed with a shaky finger and then let his arm drop to his side.

The four friends stood in a line, watching the forest in front of them.

"Do you remember what it was?" Beth Ann shaded her eyes.

"It…it was something really big—a shadow of something really big, I think."

"Maybe it was Mr. Morgan." Daniel squinted and craned his neck to get a better look.

Abraham slapped at a mosquito on his upper arm. "Isn't that the big man who helped us a couple of weeks ago out at Beech Hill?"

"Yeah, but it wasn't him." Hank sat down again, his legs crisscrossed.

"How do you know?" Beth Ann sat beside him, the others joining them in a circle.

"It was something like…I don't know. It was big but not a man."

Hank looked around for his fishing pole, then reached over and pulled it closer.

"I'm sorry, you guys." He touched the bump on his forehead. "I passed out?"

"Are you sure you're all right?" Daniel chuckled. "Don't you remember your pole hitting your face? I'm surprised it didn't break your nose." Beth Ann socked him, and he sobered. "Ow. You fell backwards and knocked yourself out when you hit the rock we're sitting on, the rock where we fish from, remember?"

Hank rubbed his eyes with the heels of his palms.

"I do, but I didn't think I had passed out."

"You did, and you never told me how many fingers I showed you." Beth Ann held up her hand. "Let's try that again. How many fingers do you see?"

"Three. Satisfied?" Hank pushed her hand away from his face.

"Hey, you wouldn't do my dad like that. I'm just trying to make sure you're okay, like he would. Don't bite my head off."

"I didn't mean to yell at you, Beth Ann. I'm sorry. You're going to be a good doctor one day, too." He winced and rested his head between his fists, his elbows on his knees. "It's just that my head really hurts."

"I know." She put a warm hand on his shoulder. "I want to make sure your vision is okay."

"It's okay." He closed his eyes and massaged his temples. "I did see something, though. It was big, but it stayed in the shadow of the woods across the river. It felt…"

"Maybe we should get you home." Abraham stood, holding his hand out to help Hank to his feet.

"Yeah, you don't look so good." Daniel started to get up.

"No, I need to tell you first." He waited for Daniel to settle down and for Abraham to sit again. "It was like I could feel its presence. Then I looked across the river and saw the shadow of something really big, not tall, but big." Hank used his hands to put the shape into perspective, shaking his head slowly. "It felt…I don't know…evil." He shrugged his shoulders and tossed a loose rock into the water.

Daniel looked at Abraham. "Do you think it's what's been killing the livestock around here?"

"Could be. But why would something cross the river to kill cows and pigs then go back across the river? That's something a man would do, I think, not an animal."

"Was it an animal you saw, Hank?" Daniel's eyebrows shot up toward his hairline.

"I don't know. I don't think so, but I guess it could have been."

Beth Ann stood and brushed off her backside. "Maybe you should tell Sheriff Stan or Deputy Collins what you saw; but let's get you home, first. I'll get my dad to come by and look you over. Just to make sure you're okay and I didn't miss anything."

"That would be good. Ma will feel better if Doc says I'm all right. You guys don't need to worry. I can get home on my own."

"Are you sure?" Beth Ann stepped back.

Hank stood on his own. "Yeah. My legs aren't shaky anymore." He looked toward the pool they called Catfish Haven. "I had old Methuselah on my line? Really?"

Daniel picked up his bucket. "Yeah, and from the fight he gave you and the way your pole was bent, he has to weigh fifteen pounds at least. Maybe more."

Hank looked over the edge of the rock to the water below. "This was your lucky day, Methuselah; but you aren't going anywhere, and I'll be back."

They all gathered their fishing gear and buckets and met on the trail below the rock.

"I'll tell my dad what happened. He'll want to come by as soon as possible, so we'll both see you soon."

"Thanks, Beth Ann. I know Ma will appreciate it." He felt the welt between his eyes and followed it to his hairline. "I guess I could have a couple of shiners from this."

"Yeah, or it could just be along the welt itself. It's going to hurt like the dickens, though."

"That's all right. I've taken harder hits. I'll see you all tomorrow."

Abraham used his chin to point at Hank. "Take care of that head."

"Yeah, see you tomorrow." Daniel started to leave then turned back. "Want us to meet you in the hayloft?"

"That sounds good. Make it after lunch." They all nodded then followed different trails to their homes.

Hank waited to start home till each of his best friends was out of sight. The noise of the woods was loud as he began to walk. Suddenly, the hair on the back of his neck tingled again. He set his bucket down, squeezed his eyes shut, and rubbed the spot at the nape of his neck. When he opened his eyes, he realized the woods were deathly quiet. He slowly and deliberately turned in a circle, watching carefully for anything that could be there. He saw nothing; but the feeling was stronger than his earlier memory of the shadowy figure. Sweat began to bead along his hairline and upper lip. Big salty drops stung his eyes. His breathing became ragged, fear clutching his pounding heart. He turned, forcing his legs not to run but walk as quickly as possible. When he reached the edge of the woods, he counted fifty paces into the open field. Then he stood perfectly still, listening for anything that might be behind him. After almost a full minute, he took off for the house. Jabbing shards of electric shocks made their way around his head with every jolt from his running feet.

The screen door slammed shut as he ran into the kitchen. Only then did his fear dissipate and the pains in his head grow less intense.

"Hank, is that you?" Ma was in the front room.

He forced himself to calm down before answering her.

"Yes, ma'am, it's me." He took one last deep breath and slowly walked down the hallway to the sitting room, his nerves still on edge. *Might as well get this over with.*

Ma finished mending the sock in her hands before looking up at him. Her eyes registered panic instantly.

"What happened to you?" She put her sewing down and went to him. She pulled him by his shoulders to the divan, sat beside him, and examined his face with tender touches before looking at the welt on his forehead.

His head throbbed, and he began to feel a little nauseous. "Ma, it's nothing, really."

"How did you get that welt? I need to get you to Dr. Warden right away."

"Beth Ann is coming over with him when she gets home. My guess is they'll be here any minute."

"Stay here." She went to the kitchen and came back with a basin of water and several white cloths.

"Really, it's all right. I had caught old Methuselah, but he snapped my line and the pole whacked me between the eyes."

Ma put a cold compress on his forehead.

"Oh, Hank. Does it hurt? Well, that's silly. Of course, it hurts."

"Beth Ann said I passed out when I fell backwards, but I don't remember it."

"What?" She lightly touched several places on the back of his head before she found the other bump.

"Ow!"

"I'm sorry, honey. At least it's not bleeding. But it is quite a goose egg."

"Ma, I saw something in the woods across the river. I need to tell Deputy Collins, I mean Mr. Pete. Is he coming over later?"

Ma wrung out the cloth and put it on the bump on the back of his head, fear and concern in her eyes and on her face.

"Hank, with the livestock killings and all, maybe you should stay out of the woods for a while. Just till things settle down."

"But what I saw was across the river. Besides, the killings are happening at night, not in the daytime."

She replaced the compress on his forehead with a fresh cloth and wrung out another before refreshing the one on the back of his head.

"I want to tell him what I saw just in case it could help."

"Fine, Pete will be here for supper in a little bit."

"I'll tell him then. Where's Jimmy Jack?"

"He's with Pete. They're spending the afternoon together before he has to go back to work tomorrow."

"He sure does like us, doesn't he, Ma? Deputy Collins, I mean."

"He's a good man who cares very much for all three of us, son."

* * * * * * *

Darkness engulfed Hank as he ran through the woods. He stopped when the trail forked. His lungs burned and his heavy breathing dried out his open mouth. *Which way? Wait. Where am I?* He tried to rub the tingle from the back of his neck. That's when he heard a low growl behind him, but from which direction? *What was that?* His feet had minds of their own as he ran, taking the trail on the right, away from the river, he hoped.

Just before he reached a clearing, he heard a woman scream in the distance followed by a shotgun blast. He was awake instantly and sat up. Sweat drenched his body. All was quiet inside the house. *Was that all just a dream?* He climbed out of bed and used a sawed-off broom handle to prop the window completely open. It was dark with layers upon layers of stars overhead but no moon. The sky was just beginning to lighten in the east. Just then, he heard a commotion coming from inside the chicken house.

CHAPTER 2

Hank dressed quickly. He had forgotten about his injuries until he pulled on a shirt that scraped the back of his head. *Ow. Boy, Dr. Warden was right. My head hurts more now than it did last night.* He took a deep breath as the dull ache spread around to his forehead. He found his slippers and quietly opened his bedroom door.

"Where you going?"

Hank bit his tongue, tasting blood.

"Shh. There's something bothering the chickens. I'm going to check it out. Be quiet, now, and don't wake up Ma. I'll take care of it."

He heard his little brother get out of bed. "I want to come with you. I'll help."

"No, Jimmy Jack. Go back to sleep."

"Uh-uh. I'm coming with you. A sheriff's deputy does his duty no matter what."

Hank rolled his eyes. "Hurry up, then." He leaned against the slightly open door, his eyes shut tight, trying to will his headache away. His toes beat a steady, silent, lively jig against the inside of his slipper while waiting for his brother. *Come on, Jimmy Jack. Hurry up, dog gone it.* When he opened his eyes, the boy was standing just a few inches from him, fully dressed. Hank's body jerked and his heart skipped a beat, startled at his brother's quiet, close proximity.

"What's got you so jumpy?" Jimmy Jack's toothy grin angered Hank.

"Stay behind me."

The boys made it to the back porch without waking Ma.

"Wait, I need to get my peashooter."

"Come on. What can you do with a slingshot?"

"Hey, I've been practicing. David killed a bear, a lion, and a giant with one. Why couldn't I kill whatever's in the hen house? Besides, a good lawman doesn't go anywhere without his weapon. That's what Sheriff Stan *and* Mr. Pete told me."

"Grrr. Get it and stay behind me."

They tiptoed out of the house, carefully closing the screen door behind them. They ran once they were in the yard. Something was still causing a ruckus, and it was getting louder. When they were within ten feet of the hen house, Hank stopped abruptly. Jimmy Jack collided with him, nearly knocking him down.

"Hey, watch what you're doing."

"Sorry, I was loading my sling with a rock."

"Oh, brother."

Just then, Jimmy Jack shot the rock in the direction of the excited chickens. It hit the side of the hen house, creating more noise from inside.

"What did you do that for?" Hank's exasperation changed instantly when the odor hit his nose.

"Skunk! Run!"

Jimmy Jack beat Hank back to the house; but Hank didn't touch a single step up to the porch, leaping over all five wooden planks. Once they were well out of danger of being sprayed, they looked back at the chicken yard, breathing hard. It was still too dark to see clearly, but Hank was able to faintly make out the distinct black and white fur of a large skunk race off toward the woods in the predawn light.

"I must have scared him."

"You'd better be glad we didn't get sprayed." Hank covered his nose with his shirt. "Oh, man, that stinks."

Just then, the kitchen door opened. Both boys jumped and turned at the sound, Hank's eyes wide with surprise.

"What are you two doing…"

"Ma, a skunk was in the hen house; and I saved the chickens with my slingshot."

"Oh, Jimmy Jack. You didn't get sprayed, did you?" She sounded more relieved than angry.

"No, ma'am." Hank pinched his nostrils immediately after answering her.

"Well, get in here before the stink sets in your clothes and hair."

They rushed into the house. Ma turned on the kitchen light and started breakfast. "You two wash up. Use some tomato juice from the canning I did yesterday. Oh, and make sure to put those clothes out on the porch so I can wash them after we eat. We'll collect the eggs later, give it time for the smell to settle down."

"Yes, ma'am."

* * * * * * *

All through the morning chores Hank thought about his dream. *What is it about dreams and me?* Earlier in the summer, he had dreamed about explosions and running for his life. Now, at the end of the summer, he's dreaming about screaming women and running for his life. After thinking more about it, Hank was sure those earlier dreams had something to do with preparing him for the news his daddy was really dead, not just missing in action in France. Corporal Charles Baker was officially declared killed in action and received a medal posthumously for bravery. He had been in the Battle at Belleau Wood near the end of World War I, but his remains weren't found until several years later. The dreams stopped when the family received the news.

This was different, though. The only thing happening around here now was the livestock killings. *Could that be the reason for these dreams?* So far, there had been two cows and a pig killed by someone or something at night around the Farmville community. Since the first discovery nearly two weeks ago, three dreams had haunted Hank's sleep. They were all very similar, with minor differences. This time the dream included someone shooting a shotgun. *Wait a minute. I wonder if there's going to be another dead animal found today? It's happened every time so far.* He stopped under the plum tree near the chicken yard. His eyes immediately found the trail he used from the fishing hole the day before and stared for several seconds.

Why me, God? What am I supposed to do with these dreams? He looked down at the empty egg basket at his side and took slow steps toward the hen house. After carefully securing the gate to the chicken yard, he checked the various places the chickens liked to nest in the grass. *It doesn't smell so bad around here now. Thank you, God, for that, at least. It could have been a lot worse. Thank you for saving the chickens, too.* Before entering the hen house, he checked the ground around it for the hole the skunk used to get in. Once he found it, he used some chicken wire to close it up and finished collecting the eggs.

Before going to the garden where Ma and Jimmy Jack were, he set the basket of eggs on the porch and washed up at the pump. He heard their voices near the gate of the garden at the back of the house. *I guess they're finished, too.* He noticed four baskets lined up along the fence. Each was filled with squash, tomatoes, cucumbers, and okra.

"Let me get that, Ma." Hank trotted to them and took the basket she carried. It was full of green onions, radishes, and turnip greens.

"Thank you, Hank. Jimmy Jack, make sure the gate is shut tight, little man."

"Ma, I'm not little anymore."

Ma took off her gloves and ruffled his hair. "Oh, really?" She wiped her brow with her forearm. "Whew. It's going to be another hot day, boys. Let's get out of this heat. How about some lemonade? Oh, and I want you to eat lunch before Pete picks you up, Jimmy Jack. How's your head feeling this morning, Hank?"

"It still hurts a little, but not so much. Beth Ann, Daniel, and Abraham are coming over later."

"You're not going fishing again, are you? You've brought enough fish home in the last couple of weeks to host a fish fry all by ourselves."

"I love fish fries." Jimmy Jack rubbed his hands together and linked them as if praying. "Can we? Can we have a fish fry soon?"

"We'll see. Let's just get these vegetables in the cool of the back porch before the sun scorches them. Then I can get our lunch on the table."

"You go ahead; we'll get the baskets. I'm hungry, how about you, Jimmy Jack?"

"Yeah."

"Okay. Be careful. If your head gets to hurting too badly, lie down like Dr. Warden said to do."

"I will. Come on, little brother."

* * * * * * *

Hank watched from the loft window as Daniel and Beth Ann made their way across the field to the barn. They had taken the shortcut and were laughing about something. Those two were the best friends he had in the world. Together, they could do anything. They made a good team—Beth Ann's desire to be a doctor made her good with science and Daniel was good with solving mysteries. He wanted to be the next Sherlock Holmes. Hank enjoyed puzzles and investigations. He wanted to be a newspaper reporter when he grew up. They had already worked together twice this summer to solve some mysteries that kept them busy, but not out of trouble.

This summer has been anything but boring, that's for sure.

Hank smiled and shook his head as he watched Beth Ann chase Daniel across the field toward the barn, then stop and wave at someone. He went to the window on the other side of the loft and watched Abraham amble toward them from the trail to Granny Rose's farm. Hank whistled from the window and waved them on up. They were all talking about how to catch Methuselah when they entered the barn. Hank leaned over the rail.

"Come on up, guys."

"Race you." Daniel was already on the ladder, climbing it before the others even had a chance to reach it.

"Cheater." Beth Ann giggled.

"What are you looking at?" Daniel joined Hank at the window facing the west.

"Dark clouds are gathering. Some of them are really piling up. Look how high in the sky the tops are. It's been almost a month since it rained. Just wondering if it'll rain and cool us off today."

"Maybe; but if it does, it'll just get hotter, don't you think? It always does in August."

"Granny says it smells like rain." Abraham leaned against the windowsill, watching the sky. "She hasn't been wrong about that since I've been working for her."

"Yeah, she's weird like that."

Beth Ann punched Daniel.

"Hey, what was that for?" Daniel rubbed his upper arm, near his shoulder.

"When are you going to stop being so scared of Granny Rose, Daniel?" Beth Ann stepped away from the window first. "She's one of the nicest old ladies in town. At least she doesn't run kids off her property like a lot of others do. Not us anyway. I think she likes us, trusts us, even you. Didn't you learn anything when we helped her out after her heart attack?"

"Yeah, well. I'll admit she's not as bad as I thought. Let's just say I'm cautiously optimistic where she's concerned. I'm not ready to totally trust her, yet."

They all sat in a circle in the middle of the loft. A hot breeze stirred up the odor of soured hay and the slight hint of skunk musk through the barn.

"Oh, man. Did a skunk get in the barn?" Daniel covered his nose with the crook of his arm.

"It was worse this morning around the hen house. It's really not that bad now."

Beth Ann looked at Hank's welt without touching it. "Hey, your forehead doesn't look too bad today. A bruise is beginning to show up, though. How's the other bump?"

Hank lightly felt the back of his head. "The swelling's going down, but it's really tender to the touch."

"Yeah, well, like my dad said. It could have been a whole lot worse. You could have given yourself a concussion, but you didn't."

All of a sudden, Daniel slapped his forehead. "That reminds me." Abraham jumped. "There's a meeting at the church tonight about the killings." Hank shrugged his shoulders and Beth Ann shook her head at Abraham's puzzled look. Daniel didn't miss a beat. "Have you talked with Deputy Collins about what you saw, yet?"

"Yeah. He didn't seem too concerned about something across the river, but he said he'd make a report of what I saw when he got to the office this morning. He said having a report on file would make it easier to follow-up with, if something like that is seen on this side of the river. But I didn't tell him everything."

Beth Ann's brows furrowed. "What do you mean by that? What else was there to tell?"

"I'd forgotten about knowing it was there before I actually saw it."

The whites of Abraham's eyes glowed all around his dark brown irises and his mouth dropped open. "You knew it was there before you saw it? That's not something to leave out, Hank. Where I come from, that's called a premonition. You don't mess around with premonitions."

Daniel's sharp intake of breath became quick, shallow breaths. "I've heard of those. Aren't people who have premonitions possessed?"

Beth Ann punched Daniel in the upper arm, again. "Don't be silly. Where'd you get that idea."

Daniel rubbed his arm, again, watching Hank through squinted eyes. "Did Granny Rose put a spell on you, Hank? Are you possessed?"

"No, she didn't, Daniel. I just knew it was there. There's a spot on the back of my neck that tingles when something feels…I don't know…when I feel there's something wrong or out of place or…. I can't explain it right."

Beth Ann rested her chin on her clasped hands, her elbows anchored on her knees. "But you knew it was there, and then you saw it?"

"Yeah. And it happened again on my way home. This time, it was like there was something behind me, watching, or…something. The woods got totally quiet."

Daniel sucked in a quick breath. "Did it get you?"

"Daniel." All three spoke in unison.

Abraham looked from Daniel to Hank. "What did you do?"

"I walked out of the woods till I was a ways in our open field then stopped. I made sure there was nothing following me, and then I ran to the house as fast as I could."

"Why didn't you tell Deputy Collins?" Beth Ann put a piece of straw in her mouth.

"I don't know. I didn't want to worry Ma. But there's more."

"More?" Daniel brought his knees up to his chest and wrapped his arms around them.

"Yeah. I'm having dreams again."

"Like before?" Beth Ann took the straw out of her mouth and leaned back with her palms flat against the floor.

"How can you be so relaxed?" Daniel shook his head.

"No, they're different from the ones I had a couple of months ago. But like those, I'm having them over and over. Each time, there's something a little different from the last one." Hank made eye contact with each of his friends before continuing. "I don't want to scare you, but I need your help to figure them out. Last time, I think the dreams were trying to prepare me for the news about my daddy's death. This time, I'm not sure what they're trying to tell me."

Abraham clasped his hands, resting his elbows on his knees. "Tell us about them, Hank. I want to help."

"Me, too," Beth Ann and Daniel sat up, giving Hank their full attention.

"It's not much, but here goes. Here's the dream from last night. I'm running in the woods with something definitely chasing me. I can hear it growling, but I can't see it. I'm not sure where these woods are, and I don't recognize any of the trails. When I get to a split trail, I run to the right—away from the river, I think. Then this next part is new. I heard a woman scream followed by a shotgun blast. Before, I woke up after taking the trail on the right and hearing the scream. I woke up this time wondering if the shotgun blast was in my dream or something that really happened and woke me up."

No one spoke for several seconds.

"Maybe you're having these dreams because of the livestock killings." Daniel rubbed the back of his neck.

"There's one more thing. I was thinking about the dreams this morning while I was doing chores. It occurred to me that every time I've had the dream, another animal was killed during the night."

"Really?" Beth Ann sat up.

"Yeah."

"They're definitely premonitions, Hank." Abraham nodded.

"Have any of you heard about another killing from last night?"

Everyone looked at each other before shaking their heads.

"Hmmm."

Just then, the sound of a motor car engine coming from the Baker yard brought the four onto their feet and to the window facing the house. They saw Deputy Collins get out of the sheriff's department sedan. He stood under the shade of the big sweet gum tree, looking around.

"He's here to pick up Jimmy Jack." Hank recognized the look on his face. "Something's wrong."

Beth Ann turned toward Hank. "You want us to wait here for you?"

"No, let's all go see what's happening." Hank cupped his mouth and yelled out the window. "Deputy Collins."

The deputy looked toward the barn and waved at them. "Hank, Abraham, I need you to come here."

Daniel backed away from the window. "He doesn't look angry. Why..."

Hank cupped his hand around his mouth. "Be right there."

They all scrambled to get down the ladder and run up the hill. They were all out of breath as they stood in front of the deputy. His brows were furrowed.

"Abraham, was Sadie in her pen when you fed the pigs this morning?"

"Yes, sir. She has her own special feed. That's how I know. Is something wrong?"

"She's missing."

CHAPTER 3

"OH, NO." DANIEL LOOKED AT Hank. "Do you think...?"

"What?" The deputy folded his arms across his chest, his feet shoulder width apart as he looked from Daniel to Hank and back to Daniel. Hank noticed for the first time that Deputy Collins appeared to have one continuous brow when he was suspicious of something.

"We were just talking about the killings." Hank's hands were in his back pockets as he kicked at an exposed tree root. "Are you thinking this is part of that?"

"I hope not; but if you know anything, boys..." The deputy glared at each of the boys and then at Beth Ann. "Sorry, Beth Ann, you too...you need to tell me...please."

"But the other killings happened at night." Daniel spoke aloud to no one in particular. His hands were in his front pockets while he looked down and his toe kicked up a small dust cloud. Hank recognized this behavior. *There he goes. He's already thinking about everything he's heard, putting a logical explanation together to work with.*

"Deputy Collins, I *know* Sadie was in her pen this morning." Abraham flexed his fists at his side. "I take extra special care of her because she's Granny's prize sow, the one she's going to show at the fair in a few weeks."

Daniel jerked his head up. "Uh-oh. That's not good."

The deputy hooked his thumbs over his gun belt near the buckle. "I know. She's madder than a hornet."

"She doesn't need to give herself another heart attack." Beth Ann squinted as the sun shone through the leafy branches of the sweet gum tree overhead; concern making her voice sound higher than usual.

"That's what I'm more worried about than the pig." The deputy shifted his weight to one leg.

"What do you want us to do?" Hank put his fists on his hips. "Let's do something instead of just standing around talking."

Deputy Collins looked behind him, in the direction of Granny's farm, and back at the group. "She trusts you four. I need you to keep an eye on her for me while the sheriff and I look into this. I don't want her taking the law into her own hands. It could be a simple prank from someone who doesn't want Sadie in the competition at the fair, but we don't know. There's no proof it's connected to the livestock killings, either. For now, we'll consider Sadie missing, not dead. So let's not jump to any conclusions."

"What about the meeting tonight?" Daniel's brows furrowed.

"Granny will probably want to go." Hank picked up a stick and began to strip the bark from it. "We're just kids. We can't stop her if she does. Besides, we, that is Daniel and I, were thinking about going, too. Maybe even Abraham."

"I forgot about the meeting." The deputy shifted his weight to the other foot. "The sheriff wants me there to help keep order."

"We could ride with her, and she can sit with my family." Beth Ann shaded her eyes from the beam of light piercing the space between the tree limbs.

"That's a generous offer, but how do you know your dad will want you there? In fact, *I'm* not sure it's a good idea for *any* of you kids to be there. Hank, I'm asking your ma to keep Jimmy Jack home. It could get ugly, what with people being scared and tempers flaring.

With that said, I'll probably take Beth Ann home first. Then if Granny wants to go, I'll take her myself. Now, I'll need to check with your parents; but I'll feel better if you three stay at Granny's and keep an eye on the farm for us." They looked from one to the other and nodded. "I'll try to get away from the office early enough to look for Sadie before I need to be back in town for the meeting. Who knows? Maybe she'll turn up on her own."

"Do you want me to help you look for her, sir?" Abraham wiped sweat from his brow with his shirtsleeve.

Deputy Collins put a hand on Abraham's shoulder. "I would appreciate that. For now, let's concentrate on keeping Granny from doing harm to herself, or anyone else for that matter. We'll all look for Sadie when I get home. It'll be okay. No one's blaming you or saying you did anything. As far as my grandmother is concerned, you're family. She was adamant that I make you understand that."

Abraham bowed his head, watching his foot kick at a loose rock, his arms akimbo. He looked up at the deputy and the others around him. Tears threatened to overflow onto his cheeks. "Yes, sir. We'll find Sadie for her."

"I know we will."

* * * * * * *

The sun began to slide behind the tops of the trees. Abraham, the deputy, Hank, and Daniel were spread out across the field near the woods around the perimeter of Granny Rose's property. Each stayed in sight of the others, covering as much area as possible, looking for any sign of Sadie.

Hank watched Abraham cup his hands around his mouth, again. "Soooooooey." He was near the line of trees that bordered the property nearest the river. "Sooey, sooey, sooey." The shrill sound echoed off the trees. "Soooooooooey."

"Anything?" Hank watched Abraham drop his arms and turn his ear to the woods.

He shook his head. "Nothing."

"Abraham, Hank, Daniel." The boys turned toward the sound of the distant voice and saw the deputy wave them back toward the house. They all converged on the pump in the backyard. Hank was the first to take a long cold drink from his cupped hands as the deputy pumped water from the deep well. Before Abraham and Daniel drank, he filled his hand with water once again, splashing his face and neck.

Hank shook the water from his hair. "You were right, Daniel, that little rain shower earlier just made it hotter."

"Yeah. Told you." Daniel took long drinks from the water pouring from the spigot.

"Granny was right, too." Abraham drank then drenched his head just before the water flow from the pump stopped.

"Okay, boys, if Sadie were around here, it wouldn't take two hours to get her attention. We'll have to try again another time. I've worked up an appetite, how about you?" Deputy Collins wiped his hands on his trousers legs. "Let's eat, then I'll take Beth Ann home and get Granny to the meeting, hopefully on time. I've talked with your dad, Daniel, and your ma, Hank. They both agree. While we're at the meeting, you two will stay here with Abraham to make sure nothing happens while we're in town."

"But…" Hank's shoulders drooped.

"It's not open for discussion." The deputy crossed his arms over his chest. He looked from Hank to Daniel to Abraham and back to Hank. "This is something the adults need to address. I mean it, Hank. The situation is already dangerous enough without having to worry about you kids. Stay here."

"How long do you think it will be? The meeting, I mean." Daniel's ears moved when his brows shot up toward his hairline.

The deputy relaxed his shoulders. "That's a good question. I'm really not sure. It all depends on the discussion."

"Will we need to stay here all night?" When Daniel responded with a sharp intake of breath and faring nostrils, Hank hid a smile and winked at Mr. Pete.

"I don't think that will be necessary, but we'll see." The deputy smiled and patted Daniel's head. Abraham's wide grin and Hank's chuckle made Daniel relax his shoulders and chest, flashing a quick, weak smile.

"All right, Granny and Beth Ann should have supper ready for us. Are you hungry?" Deputy Collins put his arm around Abraham and Daniel as they walked on up to the house. "Nobody makes chicken and dumplings, turnip greens, and biscuits like Granny, let me tell you."

* * * * * * *

The boys had finished playing their fifth game of dominoes when Hank stood to stretch. Granny, Beth Ann, and Deputy Collins had been gone for almost an hour and a half.

"I don't know about you two, but I wish I were at that meeting in town." Hank sat back down while Abraham stirred the faced-down ivory tiles for another game.

"What do you think they're saying?" Daniel selected his seven pieces first.

"I don't know, but I'm going stir crazy wondering." Hank reached to select his domino hand. Before he looked at his fourth pick, he hesitated. "Do you really want to play another game? Or would you rather go to town?"

Abraham's eyes were wide. "What about what the deputy told us?"

"He won't know we're there if we stay outside. We can listen from under the windows in the dark."

"What if we get caught?" Daniel's Adam's apple bobbed.

"We won't. Besides, as much as we're in the woods, don't you think we need to know what the plan is, so we can be prepared? In

31

case we come across what's been doing the killings, that is?" Hank stood and smiled. "Want to go?"

"I don't know, Hank. Deputy Collins put us in charge of the farm while he and Granny are gone. I don't want to lose my job."

"I understand, Abraham, if you want to stay here. I don't plan to be gone long, just long enough to see what's going on."

"I don't know. What if something happens out here while we're gone?" Daniel arranged his dominoes for the new game, then looked up at Hank. "It won't matter if we're not seen. Granny will know we weren't here. I just know it. She may know we were there whether something happens or not. She's like that, knowing things about people she shouldn't. I'm not sure I want to take the chance."

"Fine. I'm going. You two stay here. I'll be back soon and let you know what I hear."

* * * * * * *

At first, Hank was angry with Daniel. He understood Abraham's reluctance to go with him. He was protecting more than just a job. Granny gave him a home, and he had friends that were like family to him. As he took the trail that led to town through the woods, he began to see the logic in Daniel's choice to stay behind. If something did happen, he was there with Abraham as a witness. They all knew there were plenty of people in town who didn't trust colored people. It didn't matter whether they were good people like Abraham or not. Then Hank decided Daniel used his fears to hide his real reasons for staying without making Abraham suspicious. *That was smart, Daniel. Why didn't I think of that sooner?*

Hank heard the rustle of bushes behind him. He stopped and listened. With slow, calculated moves, he looked through the shadows of the woods in front of him and as far to the right and left as possible, using his peripheral vision as well. He saw nothing, but there was definitely something moving behind him. Every nerve was on alert. He took a couple of steps to the left of the trail to hide behind a large pine tree, observing the area where the noise came from. After several minutes passed and no more strange sounds were heard, Hank cautiously stepped back onto the trail. *Must have been an armadillo.* He took a slow, deep breath before continuing along the familiar path. Within a couple of minutes, he was at the back of the cemetery. He stopped at the fence and looked around. The noise of angry voices came from the open windows of the church building. Then he saw it. *Huh?* In the middle of the cemetery, the large shadow of what looked like a very large man moved quietly through the graves. *Wait. That's not...* It stood over where Hank figured his father's grave to be. *...Mr. Morgan? What's he doing over...?*

Just then, the lights from a motor car shone on the gravestones, briefly revealing the man in the cemetery. The giant faced the lights, then took three, maybe four long strides toward the woods. Hank was mesmerized as he watched the man step over the fence and quickly disappear into the shadows of the trees before anyone could get out of the motor car. *Wow! He's quick.*

"Did you see that?" Hank heard a deep male voice. He watched as three men got out of the vehicle.

"Yeah. Isn't that what we saw yesterday down by the river?" A second male spoke from the side of the car nearest Hank. The voice was vaguely familiar, but he couldn't put a name to it.

"Turn off the engine." The first man was slightly taller than the other who spoke. "We need to get inside. I'll bet he's the one killing the livestock around here." The second man reached into the car and shut off the engine. A third, much shorter person joined the other two. *Is that a kid?* They took the steps to the door of the church together.

Hank panned the cemetery for any sign of the shadow to no avail. Then he ran to the tree closest to the front window as quickly and quietly as he could. He opened his mouth to keep his heavy breathing from giving away his presence. Then he crept to the building and crouched under the window and listened, his back flat against the wall.

"Folks, we need to act wisely and not from our emotions." Pastor Bob Harris spoke above the din that filled the room. "Please, calm down, now."

"We saw it. We know what's been killing the livestock." The man with the deep voice from the newly arrived group spoke from the back of the room. Hank heard the crowd grow eerily quiet as the men's footsteps moved toward the pulpit area. He rose on tiptoes to get a look at the new arrivals, barely able to see above the sill. The deputy stood on the opposite side of the room from his position, watching the men move toward the front. Hank ducked when Mr. Pete looked in his direction. After slowly counting to five, he carefully peeked into the room again, the calves of his legs burning and shaking. When the three turned to face the crowd, Hank gasped aloud, hiding when he saw the man sitting closest to him start to turn toward the window. He waited another five-count before easing up one more time, stretching his neck for a better view.

"We saw something really big yesterday with a pig." The man with the deep voice addressed the people. He stood tall with his barrel chest puffed out. "We're from Calhoun County, down near Roarks Landing. As we were coming across the river, we saw a big man—big like Goliath—carrying a full-grown pig on his shoulders. He was running along the edge of the woods before he disappeared into a thicket; and he was fast, too."

Sadie? That sounds like Mr. Morgan. Surely he didn't take Sadie.

The crowd started talking all at once. Hank watched Granny Rose, who sat in her usual church spot four pews from the front along the aisle, look toward Deputy Collins.

Pastor Bob held up his hands. "We need to have order here, folks. Now, gentlemen, are you sure of what you saw?"

"Yes sir." Deep Voice nodded after looking at his two companions.

"Yeah. We all three saw it, and we saw it again just now out in your cemetery." The man Hank recognized became animated. "We had stopped off at the sheriff's office to report the sighting and learned there was a meeting here at the church. As we parked out there under that big tree, we saw it again in the middle of the cemetery before it ran off. We knew we had to speak up now, before making the report."

There was more disorder from the crowd before Sheriff Stan spoke from just on the other side of the wall from Hank. "Folks, let's not jump to conclusions until I've had time to speak with these gentlemen and have enough information to go on."

Someone on the other side of the aisle in the middle of the room stood. Hank recognized Mr. Miller, the man who bought the lumberyard from his daddy before he left for the war. "Sheriff, these men are loggers who have done business with me on many occasions. They are fair, upstanding men. Sam, there, and the boy, has family here in Farmville. They have no reason to lie."

"I understand that, Mr. Miller. But I still need to hear their whole story and check out the details before we do anything from a legal standpoint."

Mr. Greenwood stood near the back of the room. "What do you propose we do in the meantime. I've already lost a cow. I can't afford to do nothing."

"I understand that, too." The sheriff spoke above the noise in the crowded room. "But if we act irrationally without checking the facts, there could be consequences none of us are ready to accept."

Mr. Scott stood a couple of pews back from Deputy Collins' position near another window. "All the facts I need to know is that we're losing valuable livestock doing nothing. These men saw something that sounds like a good explanation. I say we put a bounty on this person or giant or whatever it is so we don't lose any more of our animals. Who's to say that pig wasn't from around here?"

Hank looked where Granny Rose sat and saw her and the deputy make eye contact. Deputy Collins shook his head so slightly Hank would have missed it if he had not been looking directly at him.

"I second that motion." Mr. Greenwood raised his fist like the deacons do when they say "Amen" during a Sunday sermon.

"All in favor say 'Aye.'" Mr. Scott stood, looking around the crowd.

Before Pastor Bob could say anything else, the crowd roared with "Aye."

The sheriff stepped away from his position and took the podium. "I want to warn you all before you leave this meeting. I mean to speak to these three gentlemen after we adjourn here tonight. As for this bounty, I will arrest anyone who acts outside the law and throw away the key, especially if I find out there is nothing to this sighting. Is that understood?" A murmur rose from the crowd. "Don't shoot and ask questions later. You'd better *know* you have the right to shoot before you try to collect on that bounty." The crowd grew quiet as he made eye contact with several individuals all across the room.

Hank pushed himself away from the church wall and ran for the shadows of the trail leading back to Granny Rose's farm. His heart raced with every footfall. *We've got to find Mr. Morgan and warn him. Daniel needs to be warned, too.*

CHAPTER 4

WHEN HANK REACHED GRANNY'S PROPERTY, he tripped, breaking his fall with the palms of his hands. He tried to get up, but his knees shook and wouldn't hold his weight. He stayed on his hands and knees for almost a minute, his sides heaving from the effort to breathe normally. *Come on...I'm almost there. I've got to warn them...get their help. We need a plan.* His legs trembled as he stood and steadied himself; his chest and ears pounded with every heartbeat. He walked for several feet before he got his second wind, sprinting the rest of the way to the house. As he opened the door, Daniel and Abraham were coming from the kitchen with milk and a plate of snacks.

Abraham's grin faded. "You look like you've been chased by a ghost." He set spoons and the plate of teacakes and cornbread on the table.

"What's wrong? What happened?" Daniel handed Hank one of the glasses. "Here, you look like you need this more than I do."

"Thanks." Hank wiped at the sweat along his hairline before he drank his milk in three gulps. Daniel set the full glass in front of Abraham and took Hank's empty glass to the kitchen. "Guys, we need to find Mr. Morgan and warn him about the bounty."

"What bounty?" Daniel returned from the kitchen with two more full glasses of milk, setting them on the table for Hank and himself. "Is there a bounty on Mr. Morgan?"

"Everyone thinks he's the one killing the livestock. All because of what a man, your Uncle Sam, and Clifton said they saw last night when they crossed the river near Roark's Landing."

Daniel's jaw dropped. "What? Oh, no. Clifton's here?" Daniel stared at his milk and sat. His shoulders slumped; and then he took a long, slow swallow.

"You okay?" Abraham pushed the plate of teacakes toward him before picking up a large piece of cornbread for himself.

"I don't think I'm hungry anymore." Daniel put his elbows on the table and rested his chin between his fists. Hank put his hand on his friend's shoulder for a moment.

"What did they say?" Abraham crumbled cornbread into his glass and stirred it.

"They said they saw a big man, big like Goliath, with a full grown pig on his shoulders. He was running into the woods with it."

"That sounds like Mr. Morgan, but..." Abraham put a spoonful of milk-soaked cornbread in his mouth.

"Surely it wasn't Sadie he was carrying." Hank took another swallow and reached for a teacake.

Abraham shook his head. "No. She didn't go missing till after feeding time this morning, remember?"

"Oh, yeah." *Good, that's one less thing to worry about.*

"How long do you think he'll be here?" Daniel's voice cracked.

"I don't know." Hank finished his teacake, his mind replaying the scene at the church. "Maybe those hog-skinners were mistaken. It just doesn't make sense."

Abraham sat up and looked at his milky cornbread. His brows were furrowed. "Hog-skinners?"

Daniel reached for a teacake. "Yeah. I'm not sure why, but that's what they call my uncle and anyone else from Calhoun County." He took a small bite.

"The point is there's enough game in the woods to keep Mr. Morgan fed, including *wild* pigs, without him doing what he's being accused of doing. He wouldn't *steal* anyone's livestock, much less kill it and leave what he didn't want. Isn't that how they're found, partially eaten, the rest just left untouched? Why would he do that?" Hank wrinkled his brow. "Why would *anyone* do that?"

"Aren't we jumping to conclusions here?" Daniel finished one teacake and reached for another. "How do we know they saw Mr. Morgan?"

"I don't know of anyone else that size around here, do you?" Hank dusted the crumbs from his hands. "He needs to know about the bounty and tell the sheriff his side of the story."

"Do you know where to find him?" Abraham drank the remainder of his milk and cornbread then sat back in his chair.

"We can start where he was camped when we first met him. If he's not there anymore, maybe we can track him to his new campsite." Hank put his forearms on the table and clasped his hands together. He wrinkled his brows as he thought about the salute the giant had given him a couple of weeks ago, before he disappeared into the woods.

Daniel sighed and moved to the wing-backed chair. He used the chair arm to anchor his elbow and lean his head against his fist. "Whatever we do, be prepared to include Clifton in on it."

Hank helped Abraham take the dishes to the kitchen then they sat on the divan, across from Daniel. "At least we'll know where he is and what he's doing. But we'll have to be careful. You know, not do or say anything he can tell your Uncle Sam or the other man they're with. We don't want to put Mr. Morgan in any more danger than he's already in."

Abraham leaned forward, his forearms draped across his knees. "What's the plan? What about Beth Ann?"

Hank sighed. "With Clifton tagging along, Beth Ann will need to keep close to town and listen for any information that might help us find Mr. Morgan. She can also keep us informed of the goings on with any other killings—and the bounty."

"Maybe we could put a bounty on Clifton." Daniel's smile brought a snicker from both Hank and Abraham.

From the windows near the front door, the boys saw the headlights from a motor car before they heard the noise of the engine getting closer. They looked at one another then went to the porch and watched the vehicle approach.

Hank's pulse quickened as he watched the deputy open Granny's door. "Don't say anything to anyone about what we've been talking about. Remember, we aren't supposed to know anything."

"Granny doesn't look too happy." Daniel slipped his hands into his front pockets.

"How'd it go?" Hank stepped out of Granny's path as she made her way to the door Abraham held open.

Deputy Collins waited till she was inside then shook his head. "That's one angry Indian. Let's go inside so we can talk, boys." He held the door open for everyone then took a seat on the hearth, his forearms draped across his legs.

Hank sat on the end of the divan nearest Granny and rubbed the tingling spot on the back of his neck, watching her, but avoiding the deputy's eyes. Daniel sat on the opposite end, away from her, his eyes downcast.

Abraham crouched beside the rocking chair. "Can I get you anything, Granny?"

She looked at the deputy and huffed. "No, thank you. I'm fine."

Hank noticed Daniel's knees were trembling when Abraham sat in the chair across from Granny.

Hank sighed. "So I take it the meeting didn't go so well?"

The deputy rubbed his hands together and raised his eyebrows, shaking his head. "No, it didn't." He looked at the ceiling before settling his eyes on Hank. "I...I need to ask you boys to stay away from your fishing hole."

"What?" Hank stood with his fists at his sides.

"Sit down, son. It's just till this whole mess is cleared up."

Hank sat close to the edge of the seat, his hands cupping his knees. His chest heaved with every breath.

"As a matter of fact, you should probably stick to the roads and not use the shortcuts in the woods, either, till this is settled. It's dangerous enough with the stills; but the bounty is going to create an even more dangerous situation, I'm afraid."

Abraham clasped his hands as he moved to the edge of his seat. "Bounty?"

"That's just wrong." Hank sat back. The bump on his forehead began to throb as his heartbeat increased and his breathing deepened. "How can they do that? How can they put a bounty on someone before they know if they're guilty? How do they know it isn't an animal that's doing the killing?" Hank's face itched as hot blood flowed up from his neck. He squirmed as Deputy Collins, a scowl wrinkling the space between his brows, watched him for several seconds. *Be careful. You're telling things you shouldn't know.*

"The people in the community are scared. After hearing the report of a sighting, they've decided to take action. That's why I don't want you guys, or Beth Ann, in the woods or around your fishing hole. The sheriff is already concerned people will shoot at anything that moves."

"Are you going to tell them who fits the description for the bounty?" Granny stopped rocking and stared at the deputy.

"Granny..." He huffed.

"You may as well tell us." Hank sat forward again. "I'd rather hear it from you than from anyone in town."

The deputy paused. "The description that was given matches that of Mr. Morgan."

"They're lying." Hank squeezed his hands together until his knuckles were white.

The deputy sighed. "Look, I don't want to believe it, either. But you have to remember that only a few people in town know anything about Mr. Morgan. Until we, the sheriff and I, find him and talk with him, we can't dismiss the information we were given tonight."

Hank's knees bounced from a nervous tic. "If we can't go into the woods, how are we going to find him?"

"*You* are going to stay out of the woods and let *Sheriff Stan and me* take care of this."

"But…"

Deputy Collins stood, hooking his thumbs over his belt near the buckle. "This is not up for discussion. Now, that's enough for tonight. I need to get you and Daniel home. Let's go." He waited for the boys to stand.

Abraham wiped his palm on his trousers legs. "I'll see you in the morning, sir. If you need anything, Granny, let me know."

"Good night, Abraham. Get some rest. Tomorrow is going to be a very busy day. We'll need to get started early."

"Yes, ma'am."

The deputy stepped to the rocker and kissed Granny on the cheek. "I won't be long. We'll talk more when I get back."

"Be careful, son."

"I will."

* * * * * * *

The short drive to Daniel's house was quiet. As the deputy pulled up to the drive, they saw Mr. Wagner wave at them from the bench swing on the porch, a piece of wood in one hand and a knife in the other. Daniel opened the door of the motor car, got out, and waited for Hank to take his place in the front seat.

"Clifton and I will see you tomorrow. Mom will want me to keep him company while he's here. So…"

"Yeah, it's all right. See you tomorrow." Hank was concerned for his friend. He hadn't *really* smiled since learning his uncle and cousin were in town.

The deputy waited for Mr. Wagner and Daniel to go inside the house before turning around to take Hank home.

"Clifton?"

"Yeah, he's Daniel's cousin from across the river. He came to town tonight." Every nerve in Hank's body flashed hot instantly when he caught the deputy's sudden glance out of the corner of his eye. "His dad has business in Smackover, and his mom is coming in a couple of days for the tent revival."

"Hmmm." Deputy Collins paused. "We need to talk, son."

Hank fidgeted in his seat.

"I realize with everything going on and all, it may not be the best time to ask."

A lump formed in his throat. *He knows I was at the church.*

"I've been thinking about this for a while, now. If you haven't noticed, I've…"

His heart skipped a beat. *Just get it over with.*

"I've fallen in love with your ma, Hank. I want to ask her to marry me."

His nerves shot electrical charges throughout his body. *What?*

"As you know, I've spent a lot of time with Jimmy Jack lately. I wanted to know what he thought of me being a member of the family. He's fine with it; but I want your approval, too, before I ask her."

Hank clasped his hands together to keep them from shaking. He looked from his hands to the passing trees outside his window.

"Look, I know this is sudden. I told you a couple of weeks ago I didn't know what my plans were concerning you and your family. I also told you then I wouldn't do anything without talking with you first."

Hank looked at the deputy, his throat tight and dry, unable to find the words to answer him.

"What do you say?"

Hank looked at his hands again. "I need to think about it, if you don't mind. I mean, I like you just fine and all; but I really can't answer you tonight."

"That's okay. I understand. Really, I do. This will be a big change for you. I want you to be completely okay with this. That's why I won't ask your ma until I have your approval."

"Yes, sir. I appreciate that."

The rest of the drive home was a blur for Hank. The fear he had just a moment ago was replaced with confusion, and his palms were sweaty and itchy. He tried to swallow the lump in his throat to no avail. *Having Mr. Pete for a dad would be all right, good even; but where does that leave you, Daddy? I don't want to forget you. I can't forget you. It wouldn't be right. So what do I tell him? What would you say if you were me?*

Before he knew it, he was home.

The deputy turned off the engine. "I think I know why you're hesitating. I'm not taking your dad's place, son. But I do love your ma *and* her sons. I believe we can be a family. I believe I can make your ma happy. Think about it and let me know. How long do you need?"

How long do I keep him waiting, Daddy? He waited several more seconds. "Will you give me a week?"

The deputy smiled. "Sure. A decision like this is important. You need to have no unfinished business with your dad and no regrets about what you decide. I'll be here when you're ready."

"Thanks."

"Now go on in so your ma doesn't worry."

Hank opened the door, but he didn't get out immediately.

"Mr. Pete?"

"Yeah?"

"I like you a lot. I just need to be sure I can love you as my dad."

"I can live with that. That's a very important aspect to consider."

"Good night."

Before Hank could get out, the deputy reached over and touched his shoulder. "One more thing before you go in."

"Yes, sir?"

"I love you, Hank. As much as any father can love a son, I love you. Never forget that, no matter what your answer is to my question tonight. I love you, son."

Ma came out on the porch just then.

"You'd better go on, now. Your ma looks worried."

CHAPTER 5

T HE STILL, HOT AUGUST NIGHt outside Hank's open
bedroom window was busy with the choruses from cicadas,
crickets, and frogs. The sounds were deafening, added to the noise
inside his brain. He lay on top of his rumpled covers, sticky and
wide-awake. He had given up on muffling his ears with his pillow.
Now he lay on his back with his arms straight out to his sides,
trying to get cool. As he let out a slow breath, the grandfather
clock in the front room chimed two o'clock. He was tired, but
sleep would not come.

No matter how hard he tried, he could not shut off his mind
any more than he could quiet the night critters. He kept revisiting
the scenes he had witnessed at the town meeting. He tried to
make sense of the livestock killings, the fear and anger of the
townspeople, and Granny's missing pig. Daniel's Uncle Sam had
done the most damage with his unexpected report. He and his
companions had seen *a big man with a grown pig around his
shoulders down along the river.* Hank wrinkled his brows and
shook his head. Then he slammed his fists into the mattress.

*That couldn't have been Mr. Morgan. It just doesn't sound like
him. There has to be an explanation and nothing to do with the
slaughtered animals around here.* As far as Hank was concerned,
it was wrong for the people at the meeting to jump to conclusions

without thinking it through. Mr. Morgan wouldn't do anything like that, but no one appeared interested in hearing his side. Instead, they put a bounty on who they *thought* was responsible. *What if it's not a person doing the killings? It makes more sense that an animal could be the killer.* The ragged sigh did nothing to relieve the huff he was in. *I need to get some sleep.*

When he turned to his side and closed his eyes, an overactive imagination put Mr. Morgan in a coffin at the front of the Farmville church. Hank's eyes opened as he sat up, leaning back on his palms. His outstretched arms trembled. Memories of his daddy's funeral back in June flooded his thoughts. Then his mind shifted to the conversation with Mr. Pete. He started to get up, but punched his pillow instead. His brother stirred in the bed on the other side of the room. Hank's chest burned from the shallow breath he held until Jimmy Jack settled again. He leaned back against the headboard and drew his knees up, his forearms draped across them. The deputy wanted to marry his ma. *Mr. Pete's a good friend, and I like him a lot. Why can't I just tell him it's okay to marry her?* His heart ached with every heartbeat. *It's your fault, Daddy. If you hadn't gone and gotten yourself killed...*

Thinking back, guilt had made Hank think Mr. Pete had caught him peeking through the window of the church. Surprise replaced relief when the deputy finished talking. Hank had to think hard to remember everything he'd said. Besides wanting permission to ask his ma to marry him, the only thing Hank remembered just as clearly was what Mr. Pete had said to him last. *"I love you, Hank. As much as any father can love a son, I love you. Never forget that, no matter what your answer is to my question tonight. I love you, son."*

There was no doubt the deputy loved him, his brother, and his ma. Hank had seen their relationship with Mr. Pete grow closer all summer long. Earlier tonight, when he had gone in after being brought home, the sitting room was dark except for the reading lamp in the far corner. He secretly watched his ma and Mr. Pete from just inside the screen door when she joined him at his car. The deputy had gotten out to talk with her about the meeting, Hank guessed. They leaned against the big sedan parked under the leafy limbs of the sweet gum tree. He smiled when he recognized the look in the deputy's eyes for Ma. It was the same look his daddy gave her, especially the day he left for the war. The memory had faded some, but it was still there. Hank wiped tears from his eyes as he turned to go to bed. *He loves her like you did, Daddy. He can make her happy just like you did, too; but I need to know I can love him like I do you. I just don't know if that's possible yet, if ever.*

Jimmy Jack moaned when the clock struck the half-hour. Hank lay down again and turned to his side, facing the wall with the window. He heard the distant, lonely call of a whip-o-will, then closed his eyes. He was awakened with the noise of gunfire in the woods leading to his secret fishing hole. The cardinals and doves in the sweet gum tree near his window were busy with the early morning chatter of a new day. Hank went to the window. The humid air assaulted his face with a thick wave of heat. The rooster crowed from the chicken yard.

"It's started." He realized he'd spoken aloud when he heard Jimmy Jack move behind him.

His brother joined him at the window, rubbing his eyes with the palms of his hands. "What's started?" He yawned and scratched his head. "Another hot day?"

"No. We need to stay out of the woods until Mr. Pete tells us it's safe."

Jimmy Jack yawned again. "Why?"

"We just do, okay?"

Another shot rang out, farther into the woods.

* * * * * * *

The peaceful "bob-white" of the quails' song joined the chorus of the songbirds. Ma and Jimmy Jack had already finished in the garden and gone inside a while ago, but Hank moved slower than usual this morning. He put away the feed buckets and stretched before taking the basket of eggs to the house. All he wanted to do was sleep. His yawn was cut short when a redheaded woodpecker's knocking in a nearby tree caught his attention. But his eyes wouldn't focus long enough to find it. Before taking the eggs in, he went to the pump and let the cool water soak his hair. *Maybe now I'll wake up.*

The rumble of a wagon coming from the direction of Granny Rose's farm broke through Hank's grogginess. A team of mules pulling a buckboard came around the bend of the dirt road that bordered the Baker property. Abraham drove while Granny sat regally beside him, holding an umbrella to shade their heads. Hank considered the difference between the picture Granny Rose made in her simple wagon and the sight "Mother" King made in her four-up wagon sitting on her high-back "throne." Granny was a large woman with the gentleness of Queen Esther, even though Daniel had his doubts. However, "Mother" King was easily three times Granny's size with the disposition of an angry razorback. Hank remembered seeing her several months ago in Smackover and laughing at how ridiculous she looked. She pointed her finger at him and let out a string of foul words that he had never heard the likes of. His ears tingled from the memory. It was so embarrassing he'd never told anyone about the encounter, not even Daniel. *Where did* that *come from? I really need to get some sleep.*

Granny smiled and waved, bringing him back from his reverie. Abraham stopped the wagon under the sweet gum tree where Mr. Pete had parked the night before. The colored boy put the umbrella in the back of the wagon and helped Granny step down as Hank strode to the front yard. Ma opened the screen door, smiling and wiping her hands on her apron skirt just as he came around the corner of the house.

"Hi, Abraham." Hank reached the wagon and wiped his handkerchief over his face and neck. "You're out early, Granny."

"Well, good morning to you, too, Mr. Baker." She reached under the seat for the cane she used since recovering from her heart attack.

Hank's cheeks flashed hot, then he smiled and offered her his arm. "I'm sorry. Good morning, ma'am, Abraham."

Granny used her right hand to steady herself with the cane and took Hank's arm with the other. "Business with your ma, young man."

Hank grinned and patted her soft fingers. "I'll take you to her."

"Thank you, kind sir. I'll be back shortly, Abraham. No need to put the feedbags on Samson and Delilah."

"Yes, ma'am."

As Hank escorted her up the steps of the porch, Ma opened the screen door.

"Miss Martha, you have quite the gentleman in this here son of yours."

"Why, thank you, Granny, and how nice to see you're looking well this morning. Let's take care of our business in the kitchen over a cup of coffee."

"I would love a cup of your coffee."

"Son, you're moving mighty slow this morning. Are your chores done?"

"I just need to take the eggs in."

"Run along, then. I just made some fresh lemonade. Why don't you get some for Abraham and yourself."

"Yes, ma'am."

* * * * * * *

Hank gave his friend a tall glass of iced lemonade before he took a drink himself. "Those two are making me nervous in there."

Abraham smacked his lips after a long first drink. "Your ma makes the best lemonade—not too sweet and not too tart. Even better than Granny's, but don't tell her I said so." He took another drink. "That's really good." He wiped his brow with his shirtsleeve. "What's making you nervous?"

"It's just a feeling, but I can't shake it." Hank turned toward the house then back at his friend. "What business would they be talking about so early on a Wednesday morning? Did Granny say anything about seeing me at the meeting last night?"

Abraham finished his lemonade then shook his head. "No, and I didn't say anything to her, either. What about Deputy Collins?"

Hank wrinkled his brow, looking past his friend toward the road. "As far as I know, he.... Oh, no..."

"What?" Abraham turned, following Hank's stare. "Daniel doesn't look too happy. Who's that with him?"

"His cousin, Clifton, the hog-skinner from Calhoun County, the one we talked about last night. It's not that being a hog-skinner is a bad thing, unless you're talking about Clifton Jacobs. Be careful what you say around him. He has a way of twisting everything around to use against you for his own pleasure."

"I thought he was a kid."

"He's almost fifteen. He just looks older because of his size. Daniel says he has large bones like his German ancestors on his daddy's side."

"How long will he be here?"

"Not long, I hope." Hank set his empty glass on the bed of the wagon before cupping his hands around his mouth. "Daniel."

They watched the cousins jog toward them. Clifton was a head taller than Daniel with the muscles of an experienced logger. They reached the sweet gum tree at the same time and leaned against it breathing hard.

"It's too hot to expend that much energy this morning." Clifton staggered from the tree to the tall wheel of the buckboard and sat on the back. His legs dangled at the knees. "Hank, why don't you get your boy, there, to go get us some water?"

"He's not his boy, Clifton." Daniel's voice thundered as he stood between his two friends. "Abraham's our friend."

Clifton jumped off the wagon and stepped up to the colored boy. They stood eye to eye for several seconds in silence. Adrenaline coursed through Hank's veins as he flexed his fists and scowled.

Before he could act on his suspicion, Daniel's cousin broke the tension. He offered to shake Abraham's hand, but Hank noticed Clifton's smile didn't soften his face.

"The name's Clifton, but you can call me Cliff."

Abraham looked at the boy's offered hand for several seconds before accepting the handshake.

"Strong handshake. I like that, Abraham."

"As long as you treat him as a friend, we won't have problems." Daniel crossed his arms over his chest with his feet shoulder-width apart. Hank hadn't seen that kind of seriousness in his best friend in quite a while. "If that's a problem for you, then you'll have to deal with all four of us."

Cliff looked at his cousin with his brows furrowed. "Four of you?"

"That's right—me, Hank, Abraham, and Beth Ann."

"Oh, yeah, your girlfriend."

"She's not a girl."

Cliff laughed. "Oh, really?"

Daniel uncrossed his arms and his tense facial expression softened. "Yeah, well...well...she's.... Look, she's our *friend*." Daniel hooked his thumbs into the loops on either side of his belt buckle. His red face made his hazel eyes greener than usual.

Cliff looked at each of the boys. "She's a girl, isn't she? And you like her, don't you? A friend? She's your girlfriend."

"She's...she's...Beth Ann, okay?"

Hank stepped away from the other two. His neck itched as he felt hot blood flow up his face. He was impressed with Daniel's taking up for himself, but Cliff was already getting on his own nerves. "Look, what Daniel's trying to say is we're a team, the four of us. We work together equally. We respect what she adds to our ideas."

Cliff raised his arms in surrender before taking a step away from the group. "Hey, all right, back off. I was just..."

Daniel put a hand on Hank's shoulder. "I could use some water. How about it?"

Just then, they all watched Jimmy Jack close the screen door and go to the bench swing on the porch, a glass of lemonade in his hand.

"How about some lemonade?" Hank grinned at the group. "While I'm getting it, I'll find out what Granny and Ma are talking about. I'll be right back."

He ran a couple of yards then remembered the empty glasses and returned to the wagon.

* * * * * * *

Hank stopped just inside the door to let his eyes adjust to the change in light. He heard laughter coming from the kitchen.

"Jimmy Jack? Is that you?"

"No, Ma. I was coming in for some more lemonade, if there's any left."

"Sure, honey, there's plenty."

"Daniel and his cousin are here, too."

"Okay, use the tray by the sink. We're almost done here."

Hank added two more glasses to the tray. No one spoke until he was almost at the front door. He strained to hear Granny's voice.

"He's family, Martha. He's in danger, and I don't want him to get hurt. I'm so worried and needed to tell someone. I appreciate your letting me share my concerns with you. If you have any ideas to keep him safe, I'd like to hear them. Please remember to keep this to yourself until I can work out a way to tell Pete."

CHAPTER 6

Hank's heart pounded in his ears. *I've got to tell the others.* He almost dropped the tray when he opened the screen, backing out of the house.

"Who's that with Abraham and Daniel?" His little brother held the door open for him.

"Jimmy Jack, you nearly scared me to death and made me spill these."

"Sorry."

"Just make some noise or something next time so I know you're there."

"Okay. Who's that with…"

"That's Daniel's cousin, Cliff."

"Oh. Well, I think he doesn't look so nice."

Hank was impressed with his brother's perception. "You've never met him. How would you know he's not nice?"

"I don't know. It's just a feeling, I guess. I'm going to keep my eye on him."

"You do that, Jimmy Jack."

"Hey, I've been thinking. Will you stop calling me Jimmy Jack? I want people to start calling me Jimmy. If you do, maybe Ma will, too."

Hank paused at the bottom of the porch steps and looked back at his brother. After several seconds, he nodded. "I'll try. You may have to remind me, but I'll do my best—Jimmy."

His brother smiled. "Thanks." Then he went into the house.

He's growing up, Daddy. Then he remembered Granny's comment a few moments ago and looked at the group waiting for him. *Cliff's going to be a problem, but Granny and Mr. Pete need our help. So does Mr. Morgan. We've got to get Beth Ann to help, too. This can't wait till Cliff leaves. We'll have to include him this time.*

He barely had time to tell the others what he'd overheard Granny say before she and Ma stepped out of the house.

Abraham handed Hank his empty glass. "What do you have in mind to do?"

"What *can* we do?" Cliff finished off his lemonade.

Daniel retrieved the tray from the back of the wagon. "Whatever we do, it can't be obvious."

Hank set their glasses on the tray then took it up. "Exactly. If Granny or the deputy knew what we were doing, they'd stop us. Granny might not trust us again for a long time. Let's meet after lunch to put a plan together. Mr. Pete wants us to stay away from our fishing hole, so let's go to Spoon Bend instead and talk there. It's just up the road, and we should be safe from anyone overhearing us."

Cliff looked pale. "I'm not sure that's such a good idea."

Hank made eye contact with the other two, hoping Cliff hadn't seen him shake his head. "Why not?"

"What if we see that…that big man…the one…"

Hank raised one eyebrow. "You mean the one your daddy got the townspeople all riled up about last night?"

"Yeah."

"We need to talk about that, too, now that you've mentioned it. What do you say, Daniel and Abraham? Maybe *we* could catch him and get the bounty for ourselves."

"Are you serious?" Cliff's Adam's apple bobbed a couple of times. His pale face took on a green tint.

The three friends grinned. Daniel put an arm around his cousin. "Clifton, I mean, Cliff? It's kind of the thing we do as a team— what looks impossible to anyone else. Hank, we'll see you at the river. I'll make sure Beth Ann is with us."

"We're set, then. Don't forget your fishing gear. We can meet here then all go down to the river together. The more noise we make, the less likely someone will shoot at us."

* * * * * * *

The group left the Baker property for Spoon Bend on the Ouachita River, fishing gear in hand, with Hank and Daniel bringing up the rear.

"I need you to follow my lead, Daniel, whenever we talk around Cliff. We need to make sure he is more of a help than a problem with this new investigation."

"Okay. What about Beth Ann and Abraham? Do they know what to do? I mean, what if they let something slip that makes Cliff suspicious?"

"They're ready. I couldn't clue you in until he wasn't around."

"Yeah. I wish he didn't have to be part of this at all. I can't promise he won't tell his dad what we're doing."

"I know. That's why we need to be really careful about what we *say* we're going to do and what we'll actually do. Just follow my lead, and we should be able to keep him from doing any damage."

Daniel nodded while kicking a rock down the road. He lagged behind a bit. Hank slowed to let him catch up, then stopped completely. His attention was drawn to the woods to his left until Daniel ran into him.

"Whoa. Sorry."

"That's all right."

"What are you looking at?"

"I'm not sure."

"Are you having one of your premonitions?"

"I don't think so, but.... Come on; it's probably nothing. Let's catch up with the others before they get to the river."

They ran the rest of the way to Spoon Bend, passing the others; then all five raced to the clearing near the riverbank. Cliff was the last to join the circle of friends sitting cross-legged on the grassy patch several yards from the water's edge. Mockingbirds chirped overhead, insects buzzed in the woods and all around them, and the flowing water softly added its rhythm to the setting as the kids steadied their heavy breathing.

Cliff fell to his knees in the space between Daniel and Beth Ann. "Whew, it's hot." His breathing appeared to be more labored than everyone else's.

Beth Ann leaned back on her palms and looked up at the canopy of pine tree limbs and oak branches above them. "It's not so bad in the shade."

"Yeah, well, I need to rest before we do any fishing. What spooked you two back there?"

Hank stretched his legs out in front of him, leaning back on his palms. "Nothing. We just didn't want you guys to forget why we're here. Remember, we didn't come here to fish. We came to talk."

"But why'd we bring our fishing gear if we're not going to fish?"

Daniel picked up a pinecone and threw it toward the river. "So we aren't missed if we're gone a long time."

Beth Ann sat up. "We're always going fishing. It would be more suspicious if we didn't. What's sad is we can't go to Catfish Haven, where we usually go. Fishing in the river's okay, but it's more work than at our regular fishing hole."

"Let's go there, then. I'd rather fish than talk."

Daniel rolled his eyes. "We can't. Haven't you been listening? Deputy Collins asked us not to."

"Why?"

Just then a couple of distant gunshots split the air.

Abraham nodded his head in the direction of the gunfire. "That's why. Because of the bounty, there are people hunting all around where we usually fish."

Hank sat up and crossed his legs, his hands resting on his knees. "All right, you guys, let's get down to business. Before we talk about how to help Granny and Mr. Pete, I'd like to hear about the man Cliff is so afraid of."

"I don't know if you'd call it a man, but it was big. It walked like a man, but it was bigger than any man I've ever seen. We couldn't see the face because it had a full-grown pig draped across his shoulders like those pictures of Jesus carrying a sheep."

Daniel's eyes were wide, his eyebrows stretched toward his hairline. "How do you know it was a full-grown pig?"

"As big as the man-thing was, the pig made his head look small."

Hank cocked his head to the side. "What was he wearing?"

"I can't be sure because it was beginning to get dark."

"Then how are you so sure about what you saw?"

"Look, it was light enough to see it before it went into the shadows of the woods. If it was a man and had clothes, they were dark, the same color as the long hair on his head. I guess it could have been some kind of dark animal skin he wore."

The whites of Abraham's eyes glowed against his glistening dark skin. They looked as if they would pop out of his head. "Lord have mercy."

Daniel's nostrils flared as he drew in a deep breath.

Beth Ann's brows furrowed. "That doesn't sound like..."

Hank looked directly at her and winked. "No, it doesn't sound like Mr. Moore."

Cliff looked around the faces in the circle. "Who's Mr. Moore."

Hank hoped the hot blood rising to his cheeks from his neck was not noticeable. "He's someone we met a few weeks ago who was passing through. He had a camp near here until he moved on. He was a big man, but your description doesn't really match him. How far away were you from this…this man you saw with the pig?"

Cliff looked toward the river and pointed. "We were about as far from here to where that log is sticking up out of the water there. That's what? That's about twelve to fifteen yards, I guess?"

"Yeah, maybe. Any guesses about his height?"

"No. Not without anything to compare him to. I mean, he was about a good third to half the height of some of the trees; but I couldn't say. Without knowing how tall they were and with the distance between him and us, there's no way to know for sure. I just know he was big from the size of the pig on his shoulders."

"What makes your daddy so sure he's the one who's been killing our livestock?"

"We saw him again at the cemetery before we went into the meeting."

"How do you know it was the same man?"

"When our lights shined on him, he ran; but he didn't have to jump the fence around the graveyard. He just stepped over it like it wasn't even there."

Daniel started coughing. Beth Ann pounded his back when his face turned red and he sounded like he was choking.

"You okay, Daniel?"

He nodded as his coughing lessened and his breathing became more normal. "Yeah, some spit went down the wrong pipe when I swallowed."

Hank waited for his coughing to stop. "Cliff, are you sure it was the same thing you saw on the river?"

"I'm pretty sure. He looked to be the same size; but I will admit there was something different about him, too. He disappeared before I could get a really good look at him to know for sure."

"Then why say anything at the meeting if you aren't sure? You said yourself there was something different about who you saw in the cemetery from what you saw on the river. Why scare the people until you know all the facts?"

"Look, the size of this…thing is not normal. Something that big would need a lot of meat to live. Besides, I don't know of anyone who looks like Goliath's family who lives around here or anywhere else. There's a giant, hairy creature in the woods that is killing your livestock. If it's a man, how do you know it's friendly? It obviously doesn't like civilization because it lives in the woods and hides from light. Those are the facts as I see it." The rock Cliff threw toward the woods resounded off the trunk of a thick oak.

Hank's nerves were on edge. He swallowed the lump in his throat. "What if you're wrong?"

Beth Ann cleared her throat. "Okay. While I agree this is a serious situation and being handled rather poorly, it is not what we came here to discuss. I understand Granny and Deputy Collins need help. Can we please change the subject now and talk about what we can do to help them?"

Abraham nodded. "I have an idea that could give us the best chance of finding out exactly what Granny is so worried about."

Hank felt the tension in his chest and shoulders leave. "What's your idea?"

"I was thinking about what the deputy said to us yesterday. With Sadie still…"

"Sadie? Who's Sadie?"

Daniel scrunched his face as the sun's rays penetrated the canopy to cast a beam of light on the group. "She's Granny's prize sow. She went missing yesterday morning. Go on, Abraham. You were saying?"

"Well, Deputy Collins asked us to keep an eye on her so she won't give herself another heart attack. Remember?" The others nodded. "With her crops ripening and some needing to be harvested, why don't we tell her we'll do it for her. That way, we'll be able to watch over her and get some work done without her thinking we're doing anything else."

For the first time all day, Hank's heart was light. "That's a great idea. We can tell her we're there to help out wherever she needs us—in the garden, the fields, or around the house."

Beth Ann clasped her hands at her chest. "And I can ask her to teach me about medicine. She could teach me about herbs and remedies and such."

Daniel tapped his chin while staring at the ground in front of him. "Maybe you can ask her to show you how to undo the spell she put on me."

Beth Ann reached behind Cliff and punched Daniel on the arm.

"Ow."

Cliff sat up tall and looked at his cousin, worry lines creasing his forehead. "Spell? What kind of spell?"

Hank smacked a mosquito on his arm. "She doesn't cast spells or have an evil eye, Daniel. Haven't you learned anything since working for her last month?" He put his arms up as if quieting down a noisy crowd. "All right, we need to get back to what we're here to do. Abraham, you're on the right track. I'll have to do my chores at home, first. Being available for anything she needs doing is just the kind of idea that'll work. Beth Ann's idea works, too."

Cliff furrowed his brows. "What exactly are we supposed to be doing while we're working? That brings up another question. How much are we getting paid? We are getting paid, aren't we?" Beth Ann punched him on the arm. "Ow. What did you do that for?"

"Haven't you ever done something for someone just to be neighborly? Granny's practically family."

Daniel's eyebrows shot up toward his hairline. "Family? She's not *my* family."

"You know what I mean."

Hank raised his hands again. "She told Ma that Mr. Pete was in danger, and she's worried about him. That's all I need to know to do what I can to help. If we can find out why he's in danger, maybe we can help her keep him safe. We can do this. It's not the first time we've helped prevent someone from getting hurt."

Just then, something snapped and crackled in the woods near the clearing. Everyone stood and looked in the direction of the noise.

CHAPTER 7

EVERY NERVE PRICKED HANK'S SKIN. His head itched from the nape of his neck to his crown. "Don't make any sudden moves." *That was a pinecone being crushed, I think.* A sudden, more guttural sound erupted from the direction of the first noise.

Cliff stepped back from the group a couple of paces. "Was that a sneeze or..."

Daniel followed his cousin's lead. "Sounded like a grunt to me."

All five kids put their hands to their noses when the smell of rotten garbage assaulted the air in the clearing.

Cliff turned toward the road. "Aw, what is that smell? You guys can stay if you want, but I'm leaving."

Hank motioned with his free hand. "Let's all get out of here, but don't make any sudden moves. Back out slowly till we get to the road. Then turn and *walk* away from here."

They moved in unison, watching the woods as they gathered their fishing gear and backed out of the clearing. They walked up the road until they were around the first bend. Daniel's cousin left the others behind as he ran, staying in the middle of the dirt road. The others stayed together and waited till they were more than half way to Hank's, sprinting the rest of the way. They stopped running when they reached the Baker property and collapsed onto the lawn in the shade. Their fishing poles and buckets lay scattered in disarray.

Cliff sat against the trunk of an apple tree near the road. His voice trembled. "I'll bet that was that man or creature or whatever we saw."

Hank sat up, his breathing painful. "You don't know that. For all we know, it could have been Sadie."

Daniel lay on his back with his knees raised and his arms out to the sides. "Maybe that's what you were looking for in the woods when I bumped into you."

"Maybe, but I don't think so."

Abraham swiped at the large beads of sweat on his forehead when he sat up. He leaned back on his palm, his legs relaxed in the shape of parentheses. "Did you have another one of your premonitions?"

"It's hard to explain. It felt like we were being watched or... followed? But the feeling went away as fast as it came."

Cliff's brows came together with deep furrows. "And you didn't think that was important enough to tell us? To warn us?"

Daniel sat up, leaning against his elbows. "Calm down, Cliff. There's no danger unless he gets a tingle in his neck. Did you feel a tingle in your neck, Hank?"

"Not until we heard what sounded like someone stepping on a pinecone. Whatever it was, it didn't chase us; so maybe it *was* Sadie."

Beth Ann hugged her knees to her chest. "What about Granny, guys? If whatever out there is Sadie, she needs to know so she can get her back to her pen."

Hank stood then grabbed the closest limb when everything spun. *Whoa, too fast.* "We need to make sure it could have been Sadie before we say anything to Granny."

Daniel stood, dusting his backside. "How do we do that?"

"We go back, check for tracks."

Abraham stood beside Hank. "I'm ready. Let's go."

Daniel nodded and helped Beth Ann up. "Thanks. We're in."

Cliff looked at each of the kids. "You guys are crazy. What if you're wrong and I'm right?"

Hank started toward the road. "There's only one way to find out. Are you coming with us?"

The four friends were almost at the first bend before Cliff shuffled up behind them. "I must be crazy, too. Besides, how do I know you'll tell the truth about what you find?"

* * * * * * *

They were all spread out, within sight of each other, covering the ground around the clearing to the river. After what Hank estimated to be about half an hour, he spotted the first track. He got down on his hands and knees to get a closer look.

"I found something."

Abraham joined him from his left side, away from the river. "What is it?"

He sat back on his heels. "Fresh hog tracks. How big is Sadie, would you say?"

"She's a good 300 pounds, at least."

"Would you say these tracks are about the right size?"

Hank pointed out the prominent hoof marks of a very large hog. Abraham knelt to get a better look at the tracks and looked along the trail they made.

"They're big, aren't they? And they go in the right direction to Granny's farm."

"That's what I thought, too. But do you think they could be Sadie's tracks?"

"Maybe."

They looked toward the river when they heard someone running toward them. Beth Ann slowed when they stood.

"Cliff and Daniel found some tracks over near the river. Did you find any signs of Sadie?"

"Abraham thinks so. What did you guys find?"

"You need to see for yourself. Come on."

They ran to where the other two waited, still in the woods but close enough to see the river. Daniel nodded toward his cousin, who was following the trail he'd found.

"Hey, guys. Cliff found some tracks that look like they go from over where you were to following the river south, toward Beech Hill. It could be Mr. uh…Moore, but…"

Cliff walked toward the others with his chest puffed out. "I told you it was that man or creature or whatever. Look at these *very fresh* tracks. They're clear enough we should be able to follow them to a camp maybe."

The kids converged on the impressions of a man's bare feet. Hank squatted for a better look. "This guy is big, I'll give you that."

Abraham knelt beside one of the footprints. "I'll bet he's at least seven feet tall from the length of these prints, if not taller."

Cliff wrinkled his nose. "How would you know?"

"My pappy was better than six feet tall. His feet were long, but not that long. These feet are at least three, maybe four, inches longer than his."

"Wow." Daniel's cousin's face relaxed; then he pointed at the trail the prints made, drawing the path they took with an invisible line. "It looks like this is exactly what we heard, just like I said. These tracks come from over where we were and then go off in that direction. Roark's Landing is that way."

The four friends stood and looked down river, toward the site of Mr. Morgan's camp where the boys first met him a few weeks ago. Beth Ann crossed her arms over her chest. "What about the tracks you found, Hank?" She thrust her chin in the direction of where they had been when they heard the strange noises.

"Weren't they over there, too? There's no way to know what we heard without seeing it."

Cliff started off by himself, following the tracks that paralleled the river. "I still say it was *him…it*. Anyone coming with me? I want to see where these lead. Maybe, just maybe, *I* will collect that bounty."

They waited till Cliff was out of earshot but still visible. Daniel's eyebrows were pointed toward his hairline while he watched his cousin. "Isn't that the direction of Mr. Moore's, I mean, Mr. Morgan's camp? We've got to stop Cliff before he finds him and turns him in. There's no telling what the people in town will do. Especially if they think he's responsible for the livestock killings." He started to follow his cousin, but Hank grabbed his arm.

"Wait. We can't appear too interested. Believe me, he's not there. Mr. Morgan isn't at that camp anymore. I've checked several times. I wasn't sure he was still in the area until I saw him in the cemetery last night."

"Still, we can't let Cliff go off by himself. We need to keep an eye on him every bit as much as the deputy wants us to watch out for Granny."

Beth Ann looked down the trail Daniel's cousin had taken. "He's right."

Hank huffed. "I know he's right. But we've got to be careful." He paused, rubbing his forehead. "I'm sorry. I didn't mean to yell." He motioned toward Cliff. "I'm letting him get to me. Look, if we're going to protect Mr. Morgan, we have to make sure he doesn't find out about him. His description of the man they saw doesn't fit Mr. Morgan. I think they saw someone, or something, else."

Beth Ann put her fists on her hips, her arms akimbo. "One thing's for sure. We can't protect him by standing here doing nothing. I say we make Cliff think he's not the only one interested in the bounty."

Abraham started walking toward the trail. "Good plan." The others flanked him, and then picked up their pace.

* * * * * * *

The camp was deserted, but the footprints led right to it. There were signs of recent activity from a cold pile of ashes and a pit with the remains of what appeared to be a spit set up over it. Hank's heart skipped a beat. *That wasn't here the other day.*

Abraham kicked at the ash heap. "It looks like someone was here a couple of days ago, maybe."

Cliff rubbed his hands together. "I can smell that bounty money now, cousin. From the looks of it, he could be back. You guys keep Granny company. I'm keeping watch on this place. When he *does* come back, I'll be waiting for him and bring him in."

Just then, Sheriff Stan joined the group from the other side of the camp, along the trail from Beech Hill. "I thought I heard voices. What are you kids doing here?"

They faced the sheriff. Hank's gasp nearly choked him. "Sheriff. We were tracking Granny's missing sow, Sadie."

"I thought Pete told you all to stay out of the woods. If I had been one of those crazy, scared neighbors of ours, any one of you could have been shot, if not killed."

Cliff stepped forward, a smile on his face. "We found his camp, the man my dad told you about. There can't be two people with the size tracks his feet make."

Hank flinched when he saw the sheriff's angry eyes turn on Cliff and watched the man's face turn beet red. "And you don't think we already know that, son? What do you think I'm doing out here? I don't know how things are done where you live, but I don't take kindly to people thinking they can do my job better than I can. Now run along home, all of you; and don't let me catch you out here again."

The kids left the way they came.

* * * * * * *

On the way home, the silence from everyone allowed Hank to mull over all that had transpired since going to Spoon Bend.

He thought about the barefoot tracks Cliff had followed to Mr. Morgan's former campsite. He had difficulty remembering whether he had ever seen his giant friend with shoes or not. He was pretty sure Mr. Morgan hadn't killed the neighbors' livestock, but doubt began to thread its way into his heart. He had to admit the big man Cliff, his dad, and their friend had seen could have been Mr. Morgan with a pig on his shoulders. *Why can't I let this go? I know he saved our lives, but why do I feel so attached to him?* He couldn't shake the niggling feeling there was more to all of this than the obvious. Before he could come up with anything practical, they were back at the apple tree.

After the kids had their gear in hand, Beth Ann brought Hank back to a more pressing issue. "When do we meet at Granny's to put our plan to work?"

Hank looked at Abraham. "Why don't you and I talk with Mr. Pete together today? Then he can convince Granny to let us stick around more than we usually do."

Beth Ann nodded. "That should work. Don't forget to mention I want her to teach me about herbs and remedies. It'll come in handy when I become a doctor."

Cliff snorted. "You can't be serious about being a doctor when you grow up. Wait, isn't your daddy the doctor? Won't he object to your using witchcraft for medicine?"

Daniel's shoulders drooped as he looked at the ground. "Cliff, don't."

"That's all right, Daniel. First of all, I *will* be a doctor, just like my daddy and my grandpa. Second, Granny is not a witch. She's a healer, just like her ancestors. And third, my daddy isn't threatened by Granny's medicine. He respects her knowledge, which is more than I can say for you."

Daniel smiled and nudged her with his shoulder. "I like your spunk, girl."

Hank hid his grin, but Abraham snickered. "I guess she told you."

Cliff took up a boxing stance, but Hank and Daniel put themselves between the two older boys. Before either had the chance to say or do anything, Hank noticed a dust cloud on the road and heard the rumble of a car engine. "Hey, maybe that's Mr. Pete; and we won't have to wait to talk with him. Let's *all* go tell him our idea right now."

Deputy Collins was just stepping around the front of the car when the kids reached the back yard. Hank dropped his fishing pole and bucket near the back porch.

"Mr. Pete, wait up." He waved at the deputy, who hooked his thumbs on either side of his belt buckle.

The others' buckets clanked together as the group ran up to the deputy.

"Hey, no fish?" His smile faded to a scowl. "Hold it. You didn't go to your fishing hole, did you?"

Hank was out of breath. "No, sir. We went to Spoon Bend, instead; but we didn't stay long. I think we may have found some of Sadie's tracks while we were down there."

Deputy Collins crossed his arms over his chest, his feet shoulder-width apart. "I don't want you kids in the woods at all until we get to the bottom of these livestock killings. Do I make myself clear?" He made eye contact with each of them.

"Yes, sir. Did you hear what I said about Sadie?" Hank paused to swallow and waved his hands as if trying to erase an imaginary chalkboard. "Um, actually, that can wait. We want to talk to you about something else right now."

"I'm glad you're all together because you're why I'm here. I need to talk with you, too."

Hank's heartbeat pounded against his ribcage; and he looked around at the pale, somber faces of his friends as the blood drained from his own face.

"Why don't you go first since there are more of you?"

Hank looked from the others to the deputy. "We were thinking about what you said about helping Granny. We'd like to help with her crops and anything else that needs to be done. What do you think? We'd like to start as soon as possible. Maybe tomorrow. Since it's for Granny, we're all pretty sure it'll be easy to get permission."

Beth Ann raised her hand. "Don't forget about me. I'm part of this, too. I want her to teach me to be a healer like she is."

The deputy smiled, looking at something on the ground, and rubbed his forehead. "That's nice, Beth Ann. She'll be thrilled. I'm impressed with your thinking—all of you, and I'm proud of your eagerness to work. As it turns out, I'm going to need your help now more than I thought." He hooked his thumbs on either side of his belt buckle again and looked at the kids. *He looks worried.* "Mr. Milner found Sadie. When I tell her, that Indian woman is going to be on the warpath for sure. When that happens, God have mercy on us all."

CHAPTER 8

ABRAHAM PICKED UP A SPINY sweet gum ball and rolled it around in his hand. "Sadie's dead, isn't she?"

Deputy Collins raised and lowered his eyebrows as he wrapped his arms around his chest. Then he filled his cheeks with air, nodding as he blew out a long sigh. "Yeah, she's dead."

The colored boy threw the prickly ball against the tree trunk then squatted with his hands cradling his head, bowed as if in prayer. "Deputy, I *know* I shut the gate to Sadie's pen. She didn't get out through a hole, either." He stood and flexed his fists at his sides. "That's *always* the last thing I look for before going to the barn."

"I know. From the looks of it, someone deliberately took her. That's what's going to set Granny off. The sheriff and I will get to the bottom of it, but I don't think she'll wait for us to do our jobs."

Hank looked from Abraham to the deputy. "That doesn't make sense. What about Buster? I know he isn't the kind of dog to bite anyone, but wouldn't he have barked? Why didn't Granny hear him barking at a stranger snooping around her animals?"

"Normally, he would have. He's different since the fire last month and Granny's heart attack. A few days ago he limped out of the woods with some really deep cuts and other serious injuries. He had definitely lost a fight with something, maybe a bobcat. He was a mess. After we cleaned him up and bandaged him, Granny put him in a pen, away from the other animals, in case of rabies. He does more sleeping than anything else these days."

Beth Ann looked around at her friends. "Granny needs us. I don't know about the rest of you, but I'm going over there before I go home. When are you going to tell her about Sadie, deputy?"

"Well, if you all want to talk with her this afternoon about your ideas, I'll finish my shift before telling her. I'll be off in a couple of hours. Otherwise…"

Daniel scratched his head. "Won't she think we're up to something?"

The deputy leaned against his motor car. "That's the most interesting part. We talked this morning about her needing to get some help. She thought of you guys and asked me to speak with your folks, so I did. I also talked with your dad, Cliff, and your parents, Beth Ann. I didn't think either of you would want to be left out. They're all agreeable with the idea. All they ask is for you to do your chores at home before heading out."

"How much will she pay us?" Beth Ann socked Cliff in the arm. "Hey, girl, stop that. What was that for, anyway?" He massaged the injured muscle.

"It's not about money. We help Granny because she's our friend."

Daniel's toothy grin eased the tension somewhat. "I told you to watch what you say around her. I'm just glad it wasn't me she hit this time."

Deputy Collins smiled, too. "You all are going to be a big help, more than you know." Hank noticed worry lines deepen between the deputy's brows. "There are fewer people than usual looking for work harvesting crops this year, what with the livestock trouble. They'd rather gamble on getting fast money from the bounty, than do honest labor for a sure thing. That's another reason for you to stay out of the woods. I'm not sure fishing at Spoon Bend is any safer. Just stay out of the woods, period, okay? Please?"

Hank looked down; his face stung with the rush of hot blood. With his peripheral vision, he saw Abraham kick at a rock buried in the dirt. He mentally crossed his fingers. *Don't say anything about what we found down at the river, Cliff. Sheriff Stan will tell him all about seeing us at the camp soon enough.*

"If you're at Granny's, I'll be able to do my job without worrying about any of you, including her. When she learns about Sadie, she'll be less likely to do anything rash with you kids around."

Hank searched his friends' faces. "How about it? Are we ready to go now?"

They all looked from one to the other. Daniel shrugged his shoulders. "Sure. Cliff and I aren't expected home for another hour or so."

"Can we take the shortcut? We wouldn't be in the woods that long."

Deputy Collins looked at the trail between the two farms. "I'd really rather you not; but as long as it's daylight, I guess it'll be all right—this time. Just don't use it after dark."

Hank nodded. "That's fair."

"All right, then. Tell your mom I'll see her later tonight, okay?" The deputy pushed away from the car. "On second thought, I'll tell her myself." The kids watched him take the porch steps two at a time before going in without knocking. "Martha?"

"I think someone's sweet on your mama. Is he going to be your new daddy?"

Cliff's smile made Hank's skin feel like bugs were crawling under it. "Shut up." He looked at the others, hoping they hadn't noticed his white knuckles. "Come on, let's go to Granny's."

* * * * * * *

The shortcut was less than a thousand yards through the woods between the Baker land and Granny's. Hank led the way along the trail. They were within sight of the white, split-rail fence Hank and Abraham had painted for Granny earlier in the summer. Without warning, the nearby blast of a shotgun reverberated through the trees.

Everyone stopped and looked around except Cliff. He ran past the others from the back of the group like a stampeding horse, racing out of the woods and toward the farm. The rest of them sprang into motion at the same time a few seconds behind him, not hesitating to climb over the fence. Bringing up the rear, Hank noticed the running pack was missing one. He looked back and stopped, his breathing ragged. He furrowed his brows as he watched Cliff make several attempts to climb over the rails, and his voice cracked when he alerted the others.

"Cliff's stuck."

He saw them look back and stop; their chests heaved as they sucked air into their open mouths. He started to run back to help but paused when Abraham left the other two to join him. Daniel and Beth Ann jogged on toward Granny's house.

When the two boys reached Cliff, he was hyperventilating. Hank noticed his watery eyes when he looked up at them. "Don't panic. We're here to help." The two climbed onto the lower rail and leaned over the top. "We need to grab your shoulders, Cliff. Stand up and use the rails like steps. Take your time. We've got you."

"I can't. My foot...my foot...won't..."

"Yes, you can. Calm down. We're not leaving you behind. We'll pull while you step onto the rails."

After a couple of tugs, Cliff stepped onto the first rail. As he climbed up and over the other two rails, Hank and Abraham kept their grip on his shoulders until he was back on the ground. His legs wouldn't support him; so they sat with him, one on each side. He wiped his eyes with his shirtsleeves. Hank saw the boy's quivering chin and the flashing sparks in his eyes, but he wouldn't look directly at either of them.

"I didn't need your help. I would have gotten over on my own."

The hair on the back of Hank's neck bristled. "Fine. Forget we cared. Come on, Abraham. The others are waiting." They stood and walked away from Daniel's cousin. "Can you believe that guy?"

They were several yards away when Hank heard quick footfalls behind them.

"Wait up. We may as well stick together." They walked a little ways more in silence. "I hope this old woman appreciates what she's getting from us, especially after nearly getting killed."

Hank stopped and grabbed two fistfuls of Cliff's shirt so they stood face to face. "Listen, you don't have to do a thing around here. You can go back to Daniel's if you want. I'm sure he won't mind. But I'm not standing here letting you talk like that about our neighbor who is also our friend. She's the sweetest lady around these parts, and I won't have you disrespecting her or us for what we're doing."

Abraham pushed the two apart and put his back to Cliff. "He's not worth the trouble you'd get in, Hank. Come on, we have more important things to do than pick a fight with him."

Hank flexed his fists at his sides and glared at Daniel's cousin for several seconds. Then he wiped sweat from his own brow. Without another word, the three jogged toward the house.

The place looked deserted. Just as they reached the porch steps, Daniel came barreling out the door, his face pale and his eyes as wide as his lids would allow. He collapsed onto the well-groomed lawn several feet from the steps.

"There's someone standing in a closet in there."

Before Hank could ask about Beth Ann, the crescendo of her laughter filtered through the house. Shortly after Daniel's exit, she almost fell through the doorway, doubling over with hysterical guffaws. She sat in the middle of the porch, one knee up, anchoring her elbow while her head leaned onto her hand. Tears trailed down her cheeks.

"What? Why are you laughing?" Hank looked from Daniel's prone position on the lawn and Beth Ann on the porch, her laughter infectious. All but Daniel chuckled or grinned.

"There's no one...in the...closet. It's...It's...It's..." She tried to talk when she stopped laughing to breathe, but couldn't.

"What happened?"

The three boys watched Daniel roll over from his stomach to his back.

"I was looking around for Granny, checking every room when I heard something in the middle bedroom. I thought I saw the curtain over the closet opening move. I was about to push it to the side, but decided to look under it instead. When I did, I saw a leg sticking out from under the clothes hanging in it."

That set off a new wave of gut-wrenching laughter from Beth Ann.

Daniel sat up, his face red. "What's so funny about an intruder hiding in a closet?"

"Oh, my sides hurt. I'm sorry...really. But it isn't an intruder. It isn't anyone. It's an artificial leg. Her husband had an artificial leg, remember? It must have been one of his. Daniel, I swear, you scream like a girl when you're scared."

Hank was impressed she was able to talk that long between laughs.

"I thought we were going to die. I've never been so scared in all my life. Hank, I don't know if I can *ever* go back inside that house."

"But if you didn't look everywhere in the house for her..."

"You're not listening. I'm *not* going *back* into that *house*."

"Daniel and I looked all through the house. There's no one home."

More chuckles erupted around the circle for several seconds. "Well, if she's not inside, where is she?" Hank scratched his head.

Suddenly, Abraham sobered. "You don't suppose someone took her, do you?"

Hank felt the blood drain from his cheeks as silence persisted. "That shotgun blast was really close. It could have come from here. She could have been the one shooting, but at what?"

The wrinkles in Daniel's forehead were deep; his eyes were wide open again. "Or who?"

Cliff sat up taller. "What are we getting ourselves into by being here?"

The noise of a motor car engine broke through the tension of the moment. The kids watched the deputy's car skid to a stop. The dust cloud was still settling when he got out.

"Are you kids all right? I heard the gunshot and got over here as soon as I could. Where's Granny?"

The kids met him on the front lawn.

"We were almost out of the woods when we heard it. Daniel and Beth Ann got here first. Abraham, Cliff, and I were right behind them."

"Daniel and I looked through the house. She's not in there."

Hank set his arms akimbo. "I was about to suggest we split up to search the rest of the farm. What do you want us to do?"

"That's a good idea, Hank. Why don't you and Daniel check the fields. You older boys search around the barn and livestock. Beth Ann and I will look around the house. If you find her, call out." He put a hand on Hank's shoulder. "Don't worry, son. We'll find her. Let's meet back here in half an hour if you don't find anything."

* * * * * * *

It seemed to take forever to reach the fields where Granny grew corn, potatoes, and watermelon. The two boys took turns calling out for her, but she didn't answer.

Daniel pointed toward the corner of the watermelon field. "Hey, I've never noticed that before. What is it?"

"It's a family graveyard."

81

They approached the black fence surrounding a small plot of land. There were three tombstones in the little cemetery. The ornate gate squeaked as they opened it. The boys carefully stepped around the rectangular slabs.

"See? One's a baby."

Daniel read the inscriptions on the granite markers out loud. "Arthur Scott Black, Born April 2, 1869 – Died April 3, 1869. Joseph Lester Black, Born March 1, 1850 – Died December 24, 1875. Andrew Eugene Massey, Born May 20, 1850 – Died June 25, 1920. Mr. Andrew was her husband, wasn't he? Who was Mr. Black?"

"I don't know. Look, there's a place for one more grave, maybe hers."

Suddenly, the familiar tingle in Hank's neck destroyed the serenity of the private cemetery. He stood and scanned the woods just beyond the watermelon patch. When he did a return visual sweep of the forest, a large shadow caught the corner of his eye along the back of the cornfield. He sucked in air and held his breath. The blood drained from his face, even though his heart pounded like it would break through his chest. Every nerve trembled from the deepest part of his being up through the pores of his skin. Daniel startled him at his side.

"What's wrong? You see something, don't you?"

"I'm not sure."

"Is your neck tingling?"

He reached up to rub the nape of his neck. "Yeah. It was; it's feeling better now."

"What did you see?"

Hank pointed in the direction of the sighting. "The shadow of something big ran through the woods near the potato field to the other end of the cornfield." He lowered his arm and searched the woods, back and forth several times. "It's gone."

"Let's get out of here, then. We need to tell the others, especially Deputy Collins."

"No. I'm really not sure I saw anything this time. My mind may have been playing tricks on me because we're standing in the middle of a graveyard."

"But..."

"It's too bright, Daniel. I couldn't have seen a shadow in the woods with the sun where it is. My mind just played a trick on me. I don't want to alarm anyone unless there's real danger. I'll check it out later. If there's something to it, I'll tell him."

"But you'll have to go into the woods. You told the deputy you'd stay out until he said it was okay."

"I won't have to go in that deep. If it *was* a shadow, there will be evidence close enough to the edge of the woods. Now come on, let's get back to the house. Granny's not in the fields. Maybe they've found her." Instantly, Hank froze where he stood and stared into the woods just beyond the black, wrought iron fence. He grasped Daniel's arm. "Wait. I think we're being watched."

Just then, the faint smell of rotten garbage assaulted the corner of land where they stood. They looked at one another; but before either could speak, they heard an ominous grunt coming from just beyond the little cemetery.

CHAPTER 9

"**H**ANK? WHAT WAS THAT?"

"I don't know, but don't make any sudden moves."

"You don't have to tell me twice. Maybe this is what you saw."

"Daniel..."

The sound of heavy pawing on the ground was followed by another grunt from the direction of a moment ago.

"...what I saw earlier went in the other direction."

"Oh, boy."

"Yeah. Let's get out of here...slowly. How about we back out of here and run when we're sure nothing's following us?"

"Sounds good to me."

Just as they stepped outside the cemetery, the boys heard a snort and the pounding of feet running away. Without shutting the gate, they turned and ran full out, neck and neck. They slowed as the house came into view. Daniel dropped to his hands and knees, wheezing. Hank fell prostrate on the soft grass, his legs refusing to carry him another step. His chest and lungs burned with each labored breath. His heartbeat was so loud in his ears; he couldn't make out Daniel's words.

"What...did you...say?"

"I said...I'm...going to...sleep...really good...tonight after...all the...running I've...done today." He smacked his lips. "I need a... drink...of water."

"Let's...at least...get our breathing...back to normal...then we can...meet up with...the others."

"Are you going...to tell the deputy...about what we heard?"

"Yeah...I'll tell him...when he comes over...tonight. No need to...cause a stir before...we know there's a reason." Hank stood, taking a deep breath as he wiped the sweat from his brow with his forearm. "Are you ready?"

Daniel took a deep breath then stood, arching his back. "Yeah."

* * * * * * *

Hank and Daniel came around the corner of the house to the front yard in time to see Cliff and Abraham come from the barn. Mr. Pete joined them from the garden area, and Beth Ann stepped out of the house. *Whoa! I could have sworn we were out there longer than thirty minutes. Huh! At least no one will ask questions I'm not ready to answer.*

The sagging shoulders and furrowed brows on everyone's faces mirrored Hank's concern, but the deputy's scowl caused his heart to skip a beat. *Where are you, Granny?*

"Sorry, kids. I really don't know where..."

Beth Ann straightened. "Look, deputy." She pointed toward the road on the other side of the mimosa trees lining Granny's property. "There she is."

Hank watched the deputy's face relax, then the scowl returned. "What in the world?" He trotted toward the older woman, who was almost to her driveway.

"Wait up, Mr. Pete. I'm coming, too."

When she turned from the road onto the lane leading to her house, Granny's wide-brimmed straw hat flopped with each step.

She balanced her shotgun under her right arm and carried a two-gallon bucket with her left hand. As they drew nearer, Hank saw her bucket was full of the purple muskedines that grew wild along the side of the road toward the river. The two slowed their pace as they approached her.

"Muskedines? Yu-u-um! *Ma* needs to go berry picking. Here, let me get those for you."

She set the bucket down, out of breath. "Much obliged, son. Be careful, though. Whoopee! They're heavy." She took a handkerchief from her apron pocket and wiped her face.

The deputy hooked his thumbs on either side of his belt buckle. "We've been looking all over for you."

"Why?"

Deputy Collins let out an exasperated breath. "We got here as fast as we could after hearing the gunfire."

"Oh, that." She squinted as she looked up at her grandson. "That was me."

"Granny…"

Hank snickered when she winked at him and smiled. "What's the burr under his saddle this time? He should know by now I can take care of myself just fine."

"Well, Granny, we were *all* worried when we couldn't find you." He put his hands in his pockets and nodded toward the house. "You can't blame Mr. Pete, or us, for being concerned about you because we love you."

She looked around them toward the others in her front yard. "Oh, my. You do have a bunch with you, don't you? Let's get in out of this heat. I think I have enough lemonade for everybody."

"Just who were you shooting at, anyway?" The deputy took the shotgun from her and offered her his other arm. She took it and they strolled on toward the house.

"Someone was messing around my pigpen. So I took a shot at him."

"You can't do that, Granny. You can't just go shooting at someone like that. How do you know it was a person instead of an animal?"

"I got a look at him running away. It looked like Eddie Phillips."

"What if you had shot him? I'd have to take you in. How do you know you *didn't* shoot him?"

"Look, I have a right to protect what's mine. I figure if I did hit him, he'd think twice before trying to bother my stuff again. Besides, I didn't. I couldn't have. I aimed at the *ground* in front of the pigpen." Her belly shook as she chuckled. "The way he took off, though, he got the message. But just in case he didn't, I took my shotgun with me when I picked those muskedines. Now do you want some lemonade or not?"

* * * * * * *

Supper was done. Hank excused himself from the table to go outside to think. He heard dishes clanking and laughter from the light banter between Ma and Mr. Pete. He took a seat on the bench swing hanging from the ceiling of the porch, gently gliding back and forth. As he gazed into the starlit night, he couldn't help but marvel at the peaceful picture it made in spite of the turmoil stirring inside his heart and head. He caught sight of a shooting star and jumped from the swing. He stood at the edge of the wooden planks. His hands grasped the railing as he leaned out away from the eaves to gaze at the dark sky. A moment later, he stepped down the porch steps to the sidewalk, stopping in the middle of the yard. His back bowed as he craned his neck to see as much of the speckled sky as he could. The stars were so thick they blanketed the overhead canopy with layers upon layers of tiny, twinkling diamonds from one end of the horizon to the other. The depth of stars directly overhead made him dizzy. He sat cross-legged on the grass, leaning back on his arms, giving him the best view of the heavens.

"God, where are you when bad things happen? For that matter, where are you when I have tough questions I can't answer? If you're really out there, why can't I hear you when I pray? The preacher tells us you know everything. He says that even before things happen you know about them, but I don't understand why you don't stop the stuff that causes harm to good people."

A dog howled from somewhere in the woods. The hair on Hank's neck bristled. *That's not a good sign.* After a minute or so of reflective stargazing, an idea took root. "Okay, God. The preacher says the Bible tells us we can test you. So here goes. I have some questions for you. If you're really out there, you'll answer them. Granny's in trouble because of Sadie. Mr. Pete's in trouble according to Granny, but I don't know how or why. Mr. Morgan's in trouble because of the bounty. Will you make these troubles go away and keep my friends safe? Then there's the thing that's troubling *me.* I know Mr. Pete is a good man and would make a good father to Jimmy Jack, I mean, Jimmy and me. So what's keeping me from saying he should ask Ma to marry him? Every time I think about them getting married, my gut doesn't feel so good. There's really no reason for Ma not to get married again, is there? So why does her marrying him bother me so much?"

Just then the screen door squeaked open and shut. He sat up and watched the deputy take a seat on the top step. The man looked tired. He put his elbows on his knees and folded his hands under his chin. "I'm not interrupting anything, am I?"

Hank felt his face heat up and swallowed. "No. Not really." After another quick look at the stars, he got up and sauntered back to the house, sitting on the bottom step. He crossed his arms and rested his elbows on his knees. "Can I ask you a question?"

"Sure. What's on your mind?"

"Do you really believe Mr. Morgan is responsible for the livestock killings?"

Before he answered, the deputy took a long, deep breath and let it out slowly. "I believe the report Cliff's dad made is the truth as they saw it. Was it Mr. Morgan that they saw? I really don't know. It definitely doesn't match the behavior of our big friend. Why do you ask?"

"How can we prove it wasn't him?"

"That's what the sheriff and I are working on. We need to question Mr. Morgan. To do that, we have to find him. Until then, it's impossible to know what to think."

"What if someone shoots him for the bounty before you're able to talk with him?"

"The bounty is a problem; but it's not your problem, son. Sheriff Stan and I will get to the bottom of this."

Hank smacked at a mosquito on the back of his neck. "Couldn't an animal be doing the killings?"

"So far, we haven't found any evidence of animal tracks around the carcasses. Until we do, we have to assume it's a person."

"Have you told Granny about Sadie?"

Again, the deputy breathed in deeply and pushed air out in a puff. "Yeah. She took it about like I thought she would. She's willing to give the law a chance to do its job; but she's definitely putting us on a short leash, so to speak."

"You worry about her, don't you. I mean, of course, you love her and worry about her; but you're *really* worried about her with everything going on right now. I noticed, this afternoon, after we knew she was okay, you were more distracted than paying attention when she told us kids what she needed us to do for her."

"I worry that she's putting herself in danger of another heart attack or worse."

Hank turned to look at the deputy's face. "Worse?"

"The way she just picks up that shotgun and shoots at anything outside her windows scares me. If she actually shoots someone..."

He looked back toward the yard when Mr. Pete wiped his eyes with his shoulders and sniffed. "She worries about you, too. I heard her tell Ma the other day that she was worried about your safety." A sharp pinch jabbed his heart. He turned to look at the deputy. "Uh...I mean...uh..."

Mr. Pete folded his arms across his knees and chuckled. "Don't worry. I won't say anything, but eavesdropping on her wasn't very smart. She may already know you were listening."

Hank gulped and looked toward the woods where a swarm of fireflies played. "I didn't mean to; but when I heard the words and the tone of her voice, I couldn't help it. I think she's more worried about you than usual. I keep wondering why that is."

"Well, Granny's been through a lot in her life. I've learned to trust her instinct. She gets it honest. Her heritage, you know. Her Cherokee upbringing keeps her sharp when it comes to reading people and situations. She's a wise woman. If we lived in a different time, she would have been known as a very successful warrior and a powerful, respected shaman. She takes her responsibilities as the clan matriarch very seriously, even though that role is not as important today as it used to be."

"I thought she was Choctaw."

"She's that, too. That's why she's such a strong Christian woman. The Holy Spirit of the scriptures controls her *shilup*, meaning inner spirit. Her *shilombish*, or soul, lives in a close, living relationship with God. I believe she knows things others don't because of that relationship."

"I guess your job puts you close to danger all the time, but I think she is sensing something more than the usual danger for you. Just be extra careful, okay?"

"I will; and I won't tell Granny what you overheard, either. You have my word on that. Have you done anymore thinking on what I asked the other night?"

"I just need a little more time, if you don't mind. I want to settle something in my mind first."

"Anything I can help with?"

"I keep dreaming about him...my daddy. But he won't say anything. It's like I'm invisible or something. No matter what the dream's about, if he's in it, he doesn't speak. Is he angry with me for being angry with him for dying? If you and Ma get married, does that mean I'll have to let him go and never think of him again?"

"Hank, I'm not sure you'll ever be able to completely let him go and not think about him. It's been nearly ten years since my mom died. I haven't forgotten her, and I still cry for her sometimes."

"You cry?"

"Why can't I? Because I'm a man? Son, tears are God's way of washing away our burdens. If we weren't supposed to cry, wouldn't our tear ducts close up after we grow up?"

"I've never thought of it that way before."

"Just because you lose a loved one through death, that doesn't mean they're gone forever. Think about it. We're made in the image of God, right? If God's eternal, so are we. Our bodies aren't eternal here on earth because of Adam's sin, but we have a soul that is in the image of God. It can't die. Your dad was saved. I mean, because of his relationship with Jesus, he had a relationship with God, didn't he?"

"Yeah."

"Well, there you go. He's alive in heaven because his soul lives forever with God. His salvation in Jesus guarantees it."

"I need to think about that, if you don't mind. Before you came outside, I was talking to God about a test. I just want to make sure about some stuff. I'll have an answer for you about marrying ma in a couple of days." Hank felt the deputy's warm hand on his shoulder.

"When you're ready, I'll be here."

"Thanks."

"Well, it's getting late; and I have an early shift tomorrow. Sleep well, son."

The deputy went back into the house, then left a few minutes later. Without having moved from his seat on the porch step, Hank watched him drive away.

"God? Is Mr. Pete right? I'd feel a lot better if I knew for sure. And please, don't forget to answer the other questions, too."

* * * * * * *

It was still dark outside when Hank sat up in bed in a cold sweat; his heart pounded from the disturbing dream that woke him. *That was different. If it's a premonition, what does it mean?* Mr. Morgan, Mr. Pete, and his daddy were sitting around a campfire. *It kind of looked like they were at Frenchport Landing.* They were like old friends, talking and laughing until grunting and the noise of a horrific growling and animal fight ensued. They stood but were startled by another noise. Suddenly, a large, tall man who was clothed in rags and had long, matted hair and a beard ran toward the men, his eyes fierce with rage or pain. Hank couldn't tell which. The only thing he knew for sure was the creature's face looked like a lion, but he walked upright; and he was screaming like a banshee. All three men grabbed their weapons. Mr. Morgan's rifle misfired, but Mr. Pete's shotgun fired. The lion-creature grabbed his dad in a bear hug, falling on top of him and preventing him from using his pistol. When all was quiet again, Mr. Morgan rolled the creature off Hank's daddy's still body.

"It's dead, whatever that thing is."

Mr. Pete sat up from listening to Daddy's chest.

"He's dead, too."

CHAPTER 10

I
T WAS DARK, BUT LIGHT from the waning full moon
beckoned Hank to look outside. He made sure he hadn't
disturbed his little brother before getting out of bed. Leaning
against the wall so he could see out the open window, he folded
his arms across his chest. The images of the dream were still quite
vivid in his mind. When his eyes caught the movement of a very
large person moving from the trail leading from his secret fishing
hole to the road, adrenaline charged every nerve in his body. *Mr.
Morgan.* He watched the giant take several steps in the direction
of the church. It looked like he had his arms around something
on his shoulders. *What's he carrying?* He barely had the question
completed when his legs and arms reacted with minds of their
own. *What are you waiting for? He's probably going to the cemetery.*
He found his discarded clothes and dressed before he jumped from
the window to the ground. He heard mumbling and someone
moving around in his room, then he froze in his squatted position
for what seemed like an eternity. He looked back toward the road,
but couldn't see anyone.

As soon as all was quiet and still in the room again, he pushed
himself away from the house and ran for the road. When he
reached it, he looked both ways, but still saw no one. *He's too
fast for me to catch up with him. Think, Hank, think.* Taking

the shortcut to the church was an option, but something or someone had followed him the last time he took it. *Stick to the road. Just stick to the road, but hurry.* His mind made up, he sprinted toward the church. He kept his focus straight ahead, as the woods on either side blurred past. His legs ached and his sides burned, but he kept the pace until the cemetery fence was in sight.

Slowing to a jog, he scanned the gravestones, seeing no one. *Where is he?* Then, in the moonlight, he saw a large figure move out from behind one of the trees in the churchyard, holding a rifle or large club in his hands, like he was ready to whack whoever had followed him. Hank stopped, hoping the big man didn't mistake him for a threat. He was glad his hammering heartbeat was invisible, but he couldn't stop his sides from heaving.

"Is that you, Hank?" The giant propped his weapon against the nearest tree trunk and took several steps into the open area used for parking vehicles.

Hank recognized his big friend's voice and relaxed his muscles, his arms akimbo. "Mr. Morgan." The words were breathy, but strong. He watched the man cover the fifty yards or so between them with only a few unhurried strides. *Wow! That's why no one can keep up with him. I'll bet he could beat a mule to town without breaking a sweat if he wanted to.*

"What are you doing out here so late? Is something wrong?"

The giant's hands on his shoulders felt like vises, but not painful. "I've been looking for you, Mr. Morgan." His voice trembled, but not as much as his legs.

"Come over here and sit down. You look like you're about to fall. You shouldn't be out here like this—alone and without protection."

They sat on the grass, their backs against the fence of the cemetery. As soon as he felt his nerves calm, a spark ignited the roots of Hank's hair. When he turned to look at his big friend, the man was staring at him.

"I...we...that is, Daniel, Beth Ann, Abraham, and I...wait...I thought you hated guns."

"I do. They're dangerous."

"But...didn't I see you with one just now?"

"What? You mean my walking stick? I thought you were one of those crazies trying to shoot me for killing the livestock around here."

Hank's eyes widened.

"No, my young friend. Wait here." The giant stood and retrieved whatever he had left against the tree. When he sat down again, he held out a long stick that had once been a young tree not long ago. *Whoa! That's longer than I am tall, but it doesn't look that long next to him.* Mr. Morgan balanced the stick with his open palm, offering it to Hank. He held the heavy staff with both hands, still leaving at least two inches of space before they could meet. *Nice work. I wonder how he got it so smooth? Daddy's whittling was smooth, but not like this.*

"That's no rifle, but I do use it for protection." The man's extra-large fingers met his thumb as he wrapped his hand around the weapon. "A staff is a handy tool."

"*I* wouldn't want to get hit with it. Anyway, Daniel, Beth Ann, Abraham, and I have been worried about you. How do you know about the bounty? That's why I came looking for you, to warn you."

"There are posters all over the place. From the description on them, it wasn't hard to realize I was the one being blamed for the troubles around here."

"Why don't you go to the sheriff?"

"The sheriff knows I've been away on business in Camden, El Dorado, and Smackover for several days. I just returned today and found out I was being hunted. Why is everyone so sure I'm doing the killings?"

Hank nodded, grinning. "I can think of a couple of reasons why. First, not that many people know you even exist. I guess you have your reasons for staying out of sight, but it's not in your favor right now. The people around here need to get to know you; but they *don't* know you, so they believe what anyone tells them. They don't care if it's true or not. That makes the other reason even more dangerous. Two men and Daniel's cousin were crossing the Ouachita down near Roark's Landing when they saw someone as big as you with a pig on his shoulders run into the woods. They told everyone at the town meeting about it, and those who have lost livestock jumped on that information without getting all the details. They voted to offer a bounty right afterwards. The sheriff tried to stop them, but they're scared."

"You went to the meeting? That surprises me."

"Well, I wasn't supposed to be there. I stayed outside, under one of the windows and listened mostly. I couldn't see much, but I did get a good look at the ones who got everyone riled up. I saw you, too, in the cemetery." He looked through the fence and pointed with his chin in the direction of his daddy's grave. "You were over there, near Daddy's grave, like I've seen you lots of times. Why do you go to his grave so much?"

Mr. Morgan stood and looked over the top of the fence. Hank's brows furrowed when he realized his friend watched the graveyard, just like someone on lookout. "Mr. Morgan, what's wrong?"

"I knew your father, but I've only been to his grave once since coming here. That wasn't me in the cemetery the other night."

"You knew my daddy?" His heart skipped a couple of beats and watched the giant take a seat next to him again.

The man stared back at Hank for several seconds. "It wasn't me in the cemetery. It *couldn't* have been me. I had business in Camden that afternoon and the next morning. Then I went to El Dorado for a couple of days and spent all day today in Smackover."

Hank set this new information aside for another day and closed his eyes, forcing his mind to recall what he'd seen with the lights from the motor car that night. He shook his head. "If that wasn't you, then..." He stood and looked into the dark woods at the back of the cemetery, noticing the night noises for the first time, seeing nothing out of the ordinary.

The giant sighed and joined Hank. "I think it could be a couple of unfriendly, trespassing bootleggers. Let's just say we've had some run-ins that got a bit ugly, but it's none of your concern. I don't want you to worry about it."

Hank looked up at Mr. Morgan. "Is one of them Eddie Phillips?" He noticed his big friend's body tense.

"Eddie Phillips?"

"Yeah. He's been messing around Granny's place. Mr. Pete wants to talk to him about stealing her pig, Sadie."

The giant turned to Hank and leaned on his staff. "You need to go home, young friend. I enjoy your company, but it's late. It would not be good for your mother to find you gone and worry about where you are. We'll sit and talk again soon."

"What about the bounty?"

"Don't you worry about me or the bounty. Come on, now. I'll walk with you. Make sure you get home safely. You're a brave young man, but not very smart when you put yourself in danger without thinking."

* * * * * * *

Hank awoke when the rooster crowed. He yawned and rubbed his burning eyes with the heels of his palms. The clock in the front room chimed the half-hour. He exhaled louder than he intended, but it didn't refresh him. It still felt like he had just gone back to sleep after returning from the cemetery. He instantly opened his eyes, wide-awake, when his mind registered the flash that permeated his closed eyelids. He sat up as the rumble of rolling thunder moved across the sky like a stampeding herd of horses. *Get up!*

Jimmy sat up in his bed, rubbing his eyes. "Was that thunder?"

"Yeah." Hank dressed quickly.

"You're up early."

"I want to get my chores done before it rains, *if* it rains." He tied his shoes, watching his brother punch his pillow before lying down on it.

"I'll be glad when I'm old enough to go with you to Granny's when you help her. I get tired of staying home. Besides, I miss you when you're gone; and I miss doing things with you."

"Be a kid as long as you can, little brother. Believe me, you'll miss these days sooner than you think." He started to leave, but stopped at the door instead. "Since you're already awake, why don't you get dressed and help me with the chores. It always goes quicker with the two of us working together."

Jimmy sat up. "You mean it?"

Hank grinned at the look of surprise on his brother's face. "Sure." He shook his head. *Just like I used to be with you, Daddy.* He yawned for the fourth time since putting on his clothes. *Wake up, already. At least the chores won't be slow getting done.*

Ma was just starting breakfast when they entered the kitchen to get to the back porch. The smell of freshly made coffee filled the room, but did nothing to help Hank feel more awake.

"I'm helping Hank this morning, Ma. We won't be too long with the chores. Two people working makes the job faster."

"Good. Breakfast will be ready when you boys finish. Don't be late if you want it hot."

The smell of freshness greeted the boys when they stepped into the yard. The wet grass glistened as sunlight shone through a break in the mostly cloudy skies. Jimmy Jack giggled.

"What's so funny?" Hank yawned again.

"We're squeaking. Hear it? Every time we take a step, we squeak."

"Too bad we're doing chores or we could take off our shoes and run around barefooted."

"Oh, that would be fun."

"Yeah, but it won't be this cool for long. Let's get our work done before it gets hot."

"Where do we start?"

"Let's do the feeding first. Then we can take care of the barn and collect the eggs last."

"Okay. I'm right behind you, big brother."

They ran to the storeroom for buckets and feed. When that chore was completed, they went to the barn to clean the stalls.

Hank stopped to wipe his brow. "Hey, you're pretty good with a rake, little brother."

"You're a good teacher. I've been watching you and just do what I see you do."

"That's what I used to do with Daddy." He stuffed his white handkerchief into the back pocket of his overalls and felt energized as he began working on the last stall.

"Really?"

"Yeah."

Hank heard Jimmy Jack approach the stall he was cleaning. "Can I ask you something, Hank? If you think it's stupid, you don't have to answer."

"Daddy used to say the only stupid question was the one that didn't get asked." He leaned against the rake handle, looking at his brother.

"Do you believe in heroes? I don't mean heroes like Daddy. I know you believe in those kinds of heroes. I mean, do you believe there are heroes with special abilities?"

"What kind of abilities?"

"I don't know. Maybe strength that is more than the usual person has or speed to run really fast. That kind of stuff."

Hank thought about Mr. Morgan. He was definitely stronger than the average person. He seemed to be fast, too. "I guess so. Why do you ask?"

"Billy Joe McElroy was talking about seeing something the other day that was a little suspicious, but it has me thinking."

"Oh, yeah? What did he see?"

"He claims to have seen a little kid who was really strong and really fast. He wore some kind of hood over his face, for a disguise. So he couldn't see exactly who he was, but he also had a cape around his neck and called himself the Golden Eagle."

For several seconds neither spoke. *Aw, Hank. Just go with him on this. It's not like it's dangerous to encourage his imagination.* "The Golden Eagle? What's that? Some kind of secret identity or something?"

"That's what Billy Joe said. Then Otis said he saw the same thing. The kid was strong because he could break a thick tree limb with his bare hands. You know, without using his knee. And he could climb to the top of a tree as fast as a bird could fly."

"What do *you* think? Do you believe him?"

Jimmy Jack looked up as if he were seeing the possibilities. "I think it's possible. After all, Samson was really strong. You know? Samson from the Bible? I don't know anyone who is really fast, but I guess it could happen if God wanted someone to be."

Hank went back to work. "Well, then, there's your answer. It doesn't really matter what I think."

"But it does. You're the bravest person I know, except for maybe Mr. Pete. I think you're a hero, and I know I want to be a hero just like you are. You helped Abraham and his family. You even sort of helped Pinky from Snow Hill. You help Granny Rose all the time and don't even think about it before you volunteer. Mr. Pete thinks you're pretty special because you aren't afraid to do what needs to be done, and you don't make a fuss about it. He says he respects you because you know when to back off and let him and Sheriff Stan take over. I want Mr. Pete to say those kinds of things about me, too. I told him I want to be a lawman just like him when I grow up. He's teaching me things already when he takes me with him places and says you can teach me things, too. I can't wait for him to ask Ma to marry him. I want them to get married as soon after he asks her as they can."

Hank held the rake still for a moment as a pain stabbed his heart at the mention of a wedding. "Mr. Pete really said those things?" He slowly finished cleaning the stall then looked at Jimmy Jack, leaning on the rake handle.

"Yeah."

"Are you ready to collect the eggs and go in for breakfast?"

"Yep."

"Good. I'm finished, too."

After they put the rakes away and closed the barn, they went to the storeroom for the egg baskets and ran to finish the last chore. Hank was lost in thought about how the Golden Eagle could break a tree limb without using his knee when Jimmy Jack yelled from the yard. It took everything in him to keep his basket balanced and upright before splattering raw eggs all over the hen house. He ran out the door and saw his brother near the fence at the back of the chicken yard. He carefully set the basket of eggs on top of the coop under the shade of the mulberry tree.

"What's wrong?"

"Look." He pointed at the ground on the other side of the wire fence.

Hank knelt down to get a closer look at the undeniably large cat track in the soft mud.

CHAPTER 11

THE HAIR ON THE BACK of Hank's neck bristled; his heart pounded. He looked around the perimeter of the farm and then at the branches in the tree overhead. *Nothing.* He blew out a sharp breath and wiped his brow. *Thank you, God!*

Jimmy Jack knelt beside his brother. "That's from a cat, isn't it? A big one."

"Yeah, it's a big cat, all right. Finish collecting the eggs. I'm going to see if there are more tracks, see if I can tell where they came from and where they go from here." He grabbed the fence wire to stand and forced himself to walk as he left the chicken yard and looked for more prints. He searched in both directions from the clear track his brother had found. When he saw the second, third, fourth, and fifth paw impressions in the mud, leading to the trail he used to get to his fishing hole, every hair follicle on his head tingled. He rubbed his forearms and shivered. Goose bumps caused the hairs on his arms to stand up. *Hey, wait a minute. These tracks were made after it rained. This cat was here while we were doing our chores. Maybe watching us get started. Why didn't we hear the chickens raise a fuss?*

He stood and studied the woods for several minutes, his fingers tapping a nervous rhythm on his legs. Suddenly, his mind ignited a spark of realization, his thoughts rushing to make the pieces of recent events fit. *Whoa, this could be what's been killing the livestock around here, couldn't it? I* knew *it was possible an animal was causing the panic—not Mr. Morgan or any other man, for that matter. The question now is how to convince everyone else.*

The touch on his shoulder startled him out of his reverie. He instinctively swung his leg, kicking as he turned around and plowed his foot into Jimmy Jack's midsection. "Hey!"

"Jimmy! I'm so sorry." Hank reached out to help his brother up off the ground. "You scared me."

"I figured that. What did you find?" He scrunched his face as he wiped the mud from his hands on his trousers and checked his backside.

"As best I can tell, it went into the woods, toward the fishing hole, after being outside the chicken yard." He pointed out the path the cat took. "See? It doesn't seem to be in a hurry."

"I know you're smart and all about these kinds of things, but how can you tell?"

"The distance between the tracks is too uniform for it to be running. If it were running, there would be more space between the tracks at times. These all measure about the same between each other."

"Wow!"

"The pattern is different from running tracks, too."

"What do we do now? Do we tell Ma? Maybe we should tell Mr. Pete."

"Yeah. Let's tell Mr. Pete first, when he comes by to take me to Granny's. Maybe *he'll* tell Ma so she's not worried or upset."

"Okay. Do you think it's still out there?"

Hank watched the woods again. "Definitely, but I think it's out of the area right now." *I hope, anyway.*

"Will it come back?"

"I don't know. If I had to guess, I'd say it's probably just looking around. It's not hungry or else it would have eaten something." *That's it! It eats what it wants and leaves the rest. That's why the dead animals are found the way they are. It gets full and leaves the rest for later, but isn't able to finish it off because the owners bury or burn them. All of the animals that have been killed were found in open fields. The grass covers the cat's tracks!*

"What's wrong? Do you see it out there?"

"No. Just thinking. Let's get back to the house before Ma gets worried. Did you finish collecting the eggs?"

"Yeah. I put my basket beside yours on the chicken coop."

"My stomach's rumbling." He rubbed his belly, closed his eyes, and sniffed. "I can smell the bacon and sausage from out here. Come on, I'll race you to the back porch."

"Okay, go!" Jimmy Jack took off running. "Don't forget the eggs!"

"Hey, no fair! You can't have a head start!" His brother just giggled.

* * * * * * *

Deputy Collins arrived at the Bakers' house just as everyone was finishing up breakfast. He came to the back porch screen door.

"Knock-knock!"

Ma greeted him as he entered the kitchen. "Pete! Come in!" Hank noticed the bounce in her step. His pulse reverberated in his ears, wondering why he still balked at the deputy's desire to marry his mother. "You're just in time for what's left over after these two hungry bears ate. They worked up quite an appetite doing chores together, coming in laughing and excited about something."

"Mr. Pete!" Jimmy Jack rushed to the man, nearly knocking him over, throwing his arms around the deputy's legs.

"Whoa, there!" He kissed Ma on the cheek; and then knelt to give Jimmy a tight, tickling squeeze that made him giggle long, hard, and loud. Hank couldn't help but smile as his little brother wriggled and writhed in the big man's strong grip, unable to escape. After a couple of minutes, he let Jimmy go and stood, still grinning. "Thanks, Martha, but I've already eaten. I just came by to pick up Hank. I'll be picking up the others then getting them all to Granny's at the same time. The sooner the kids get there, the sooner they will finish today's list. I have to tell you, I'm glad I work for Stan."

"Sounds like they're in for a full day."

"I'll get them home in time for evening chores and supper."

"I hope they're not too tired to do chores when they get home."

"Granny won't let them get that tired. Are you ready, son?"

Hank took one more drink of milk, then stood to leave. "Yes, sir."

Ma hugged Mr. Pete one more time. "Why don't you stay for supper tonight—fried catfish, hush puppies, and fresh collard greens."

"Now that's an offer I can't refuse. I'll take the other kids home first." He kissed Ma again, then held the door open for Hank. "Let's go, son. The sheriff and I have a busy morning ahead."

"See you later, Jimmy, Ma."

"Bye, son. Have a good day."

They were almost to the motor car when the screen door slammed shut. "Hank! Wait up!" They watched the boy jump off the porch and run toward them. He was out of breath, but had enough air to be understood. "I didn't want to say anything around Ma. What about the cat?"

"Oh, yeah. I almost forgot."

"What cat?" The deputy's brows furrowed as he looked from one brother to the other.

Hank swatted at a horsefly buzzing around his head. "When we were doing chores this morning, Jimmy saw a cat track near the chicken yard in the mud. It had been here sometime after the rain stopped; but we didn't see it, just the paw print. There are more tracks that go toward the trail in the woods over there." He pointed out each of the sites as he mentioned them. "It looks like a really big cat, too." He rested his hands on his hips, his arms akimbo.

The deputy crossed his arms over his chest, his feet shoulder-width apart. "Are you sure it's a cat's track?"

"Yes, sir. Daddy used to find them all the time and point them out to me. But I have to tell you, I've never seen any the size of these."

The deputy started to go toward the chicken yard, but hesitated. Then he put a hand on each of the boys' shoulders. "Jimmy Jack, you go back inside. You boys did the right thing telling me about this. Your ma needs to know, but maybe I should be the one to tell her."

"Hank hoped you'd tell her. He didn't want to upset her. Besides, this is a job for us men to handle. I remember what you taught me about how a good lawman is prepared for anything. I'm keeping my peashooter close by, just in case it comes back."

"Now, hold on, Jimmy Jack. A good lawman also knows when to act alone and when to wait for help. Don't you go doing anything by yourself that could get your ma, your brother, or you hurt."

"I won't. But I've thought about what you said about how you keep your weapon ready at all times for when it may be needed. That's what I'm doing."

The deputy smiled. "Okay, but I mean it. Don't go shooting that peashooter at an animal with a bad temper. Now, go on back inside, son. Hank, show me those tracks."

* * * * * * *

As the deputy studied the ground, Hank admired his tenacity with the details. He watched him draw pencil sketches in the little notebook he always carried when he was on duty. He used a clean sheet for each individual track and made sure they were identical before standing to leave.

"You draw really well. Is that something you learned to do at the police school?"

"No. My father told me everyone has a special gift. He said mine is drawing. It comes naturally to me. He was a lawman, too, you know. When I took an interest in the law, he taught me some of the skills that made him the best investigator in his jurisdiction. As he looked at crime scenes, he took in every detail, making a picture in his mind. That was his special gift. He *never* forgot anything he saw. I don't have that skill, but he showed me how to use my drawing skills to do the same thing his mind did naturally."

"May I see the drawings you just did?"

The deputy handed the notepad to him. "Sure."

Hank compared the drawings to the tracks, seeing no difference in them at all. "You're good." He handed the book back to Mr. Pete.

"I have all I need. Let's get out of here before your ma gets curious and starts wondering what we're doing." They walked back to the motor car and got in. "I'll show these to the sheriff, and we'll get right on it. I appreciate your being mature about all this business. That's the sign of a man, you know." He paused long enough for them to get settled in the car. "I think it's time to share something with you." He started the engine and drove down the lane between the house and the road.

Hank looked out the side window. *Please don't try to get me to agree to let you marry Ma just because you think I'm mature.*

"The sheriff and I have been considering the idea that an animal could be killing the livestock. Both of us have felt that way from the beginning." Hank jerked his head around to look at the deputy. "We just needed proof there was something big enough in the area to do such a thing, but we couldn't get it. Your finding these tracks is just what we've been waiting for. This could be the key to making everyone sit up and listen to us. We never believed Mr. Morgan was guilty, not even after Cliff's father and friend spoke to the sheriff. With this, you've given us the proof we needed. We had considered that some sort of wildcat was the real culprit. From the size of these tracks, I'd say we're looking for a very large panther."

Hank looked out the front window without seeing anything. He considered what all this meant and the possible connection with the screams in his recent reoccurring dreams and furrowed his brows. "Does a panther ever sound like a woman screaming? I mean, I know it growls and has a distinct roar; but does it ever sound like that?"

"As a matter of fact, it can. Why do you ask? Have you heard it?"

"I'm not sure. I have dreams sometimes that seem real, but I can never be sure. I keep having one dream, over and over, that seems to always occur on the nights when another animal has been killed. The last two had the sound of a woman screaming in them. When I woke up, I wasn't sure if any of it was real."

"You have dreams, do you?"

"Yes, sir."

"You know, having those kinds of dreams, the ones that appear to predict events, is what a lot of Indians call powerful medicine." The deputy grinned.

Hank looked over at the man and smiled in spite of the seriousness of the conversation. "Really?"

"You'd have the respect of a lot of people. Why haven't you mentioned these dreams before?"

"I never thought of them as anything important. They scare Daniel."

"Don't take this wrong because I like him a lot; but it doesn't take much to scare Daniel, does it?"

"No, sir." They both snickered.

As the deputy turned off the road leading to the Wagner house, they saw Daniel and Cliff waving from the porch steps. "Let's hold off on talking too much about the cat right now. Give me time to talk with the sheriff before we make it public knowledge."

"Yes, sir."

* * * * * * *

The drive to Granny's after picking up Beth Ann took only a few minutes, but it felt like hours to Hank. He couldn't wait to be alone with Daniel to tell him what had happened this morning. After all, they were partners, practically twins who knew what each was thinking anyway. He'll know something important had happened. What harm could it do to let him in on the tracks he and Jimmy had found? He'd wait to say anything about what Mr. Pete had shared about his and the sheriff's suspicions, like the deputy had requested. It won't be long before the whole area knows they've been hunting an innocent man.

Just as Granny's house came into view, Cliff leaned forward from the back seat, his arm stretched toward the windshield between the deputy and Beth Ann, pointing. His voice cracked. "That's him! That's the man we saw when we crossed the river! Arrest him, deputy! That's the man who's been killing the livestock around here!"

In the front yard, laughing with Granny and Abraham was Mr. Morgan.

CHAPTER 12

THE DEPUTY TURNED AROUND IN his seat to look at Cliff.
"Now hold on. I'm not arresting anyone. I need positive proof
he's the one doing the killing. Just because you say you saw him
with a pig on his shoulders does not make him guilty of anything."

"I'll go to the sheriff, then." Daniel's cousin sat back hard with
his arms folded across his heaving chest. The hard look in his eyes
and his flaring nostrils lit a fire in Hank's heart.

Deputy Collins let out a loud sigh; then he turned around in
his seat, looking at Cliff. "You do what you feel you have to do,
and so will I. You're sure this man has committed these crimes,
but I'm not. So let's give him an opportunity to tell his side of
the story, shall we? But I'm warning you; don't leave this vehicle
half-cocked and ready to destroy a man's reputation without
just cause. Now calm down, and let's do this the right way." No
one said a word for several seconds. The deputy reached across
Beth Ann and opened the door for her before stepping out of
the motor car himself. He let all the boys out the back door
before he stopped Cliff with a grip on the boy's upper arm. Then
Deputy Collins used his other hand to point at Daniel's cousin's
nose. "Don't say a word unless I ask you a direct question.
Understand?" Cliff nodded. "I want you to listen to every word
that's said so you hear everything clearly."

Hank shook his head, shaking his senses from a feeling of *déjà vu* while watching the exchange. *He acts so much like you, Daddy. It's like watching you, but it's not you.* His pulse raced when he acknowledged a respect that had once been reserved for his father. Now it was for Mr. Pete and his ability to challenge Cliff in a controlled and professional manner. *That's the kind of man who will teach you well, son, and do right by your mother, Jimmy Jack, and you.* Hank's heart skipped a beat. *Daddy?* It had been quite a while since hearing his father speak so clearly to him. He had almost forgotten what his hero-father had sounded like until he witnessed the exchange between Mr. Pete and Cliff. His heart ached and welled up with pride and excitement. He felt a warm hand on his shoulder, bursting the bubble of nostalgia.

Daniel came into conscious view. "You all right? You look a hundred miles away." His eyes searched Hank's face, his brows almost touching as they came together. "You're going to miss Deputy Collins showing Cliff just how wrong he is about Mr. Morgan."

He looked to his left then right, turning in a circle to get his bearings, feeling like he'd just awakened from a sound sleep, wondering how he had arrived here. "Sorry. I was thinking or..."

Daniel got behind him. "Well, stop it. Snap out of it and come on." He pushed Hank toward the porch. "You're going to make me miss the best comeuppance for Cliff's smart-mouthing I've ever seen, thanks to the deputy. Have I told you lately what a great guy he is?"

As they closed in on the pending confrontation, everyone else had already taken their places. Beth Ann sat next to Granny on the hanging bench-swing on her front porch. They were apart from where the real action would happen, but still able to observe everything. Mr. Morgan sat on the edge of the porch on the opposite side from the swing, leaning against the corner post. Mr. Pete and Cliff stood a few feet away from the giant, at eye level with the big man. Hank realized the deputy had introduced Cliff to Mr. Morgan when the big man reached to shake hands, but Daniel's cousin waited several seconds before complying with the deputy's gentle prodding. Hank and Daniel sat near Abraham in the middle of the porch on the top step. Daniel was clearly excited as a sinister smile crossed his face.

"This is going to be good." Daniel rubbed his hands together before resting his elbows on his knees, clasping his hands in the space between them.

"Jeffrey, would you mind answering some questions for me so our friend, here, can get to know you?"

Before the giant answered, he shifted his position against the post so his arms wrapped around the raised knee that had been stretched out in front of him before. Hank remembered what the deputy had told him about a good investigator's ability to read people. *The key is to watch the body language as well as the face and eyes. Everything* about *a person speaks of the person: words spoken, demeanor, unconscious facial signals, hand positions, stance.* Hank practiced his skills at reading this situation as he took note of his observations. Cliff crossed his arms over his chest, as tense as his big friend and Mr. Pete were relaxed.

"How often do you come around here?"

Mr. Morgan looked at Granny and smiled. "I come over here almost everyday when I'm in the area." He nodded toward Granny. "She makes me brains and scrambled eggs for breakfast and liver and onions for lunch in exchange for helping Abraham by doing odd jobs around the place."

Daniel broke Hank's concentration momentarily. "Now that's just nasty. My ma made me eat that for breakfast once, but I couldn't make it go down. My throat wouldn't let it. And liver and onions?" The gagging sound made Hank snicker. "That's just a terrible waste of perfectly good eggs and onions, if you ask me."

"What's wrong with brains and liver? I happen to like both."

Daniel just stared at him. "And to think I've taken a drink from your well with the same dipper *your* mouth has touched all this time."

"Yeah." Hank smiled and nudged his best friend's shoulder. "Now be quiet. I'm trying to listen to this."

"She told me the kids were helping her out for the next several days; so I decided to stay and lend a hand, too. Some of those watermelons of hers are as big as small boulders, you know." Mr. Morgan, Granny, and Mr. Pete chuckled.

"Why haven't we seen you around lately, Jeffrey?"

"Well, I like to stay to myself mostly. After being in the war, it's hard to be around loud noises and lots of people without feeling like I'm back there in it, again. So I live in the woods for the most part. Granny lets me bunk with Abraham when it's wet or cold. But you asked about recently. I had business in Camden, El Dorado, and then Smackover that took nigh on to a week to complete. I just returned yesterday."

"Did you go to Miller's Bluff or Roark's Landing while you were out and about?"

Mr. Morgan shook his head. "No. Just Camden, El Dorado, and Smackover."

Cliff dropped his hands, making fists that bore white knuckles. "He's lying."

The giant jerked his head to look directly at the boy. Hank noticed the deputy start to say something, but Mr. Morgan kept him silent with an outstretched arm. The big man's Adam's apple bobbed a couple of times. Hank almost missed the slight quiver of his chin as his tight lips closed over his clenched teeth, then he noticed the big vein in the giant's neck was more defined. *That was the wrong thing to say.*

Daniel tensed beside Hank, sitting without the slouch of a moment ago. "Oooo!"

"Son, I am a lot of things and done a lot of things I'm not proud of; but I am *not* a liar." The big man changed his posture to face Cliff, wrapping his hands over his knees. His feet were flat on the ground nearly four feet from the top of the porch, his legs in a perfect ninety-degree angle. Then he closed his eyes and took a slow breath, in and out. "I understand you and your dad and a friend think you saw me near the river, but I'd like to hear you describe exactly what you saw."

The deputy crossed his arms over his chest, looking at Cliff. "That's a good idea."

Daniel's cousin put his hands on his hips and watched his foot kick at the fast-drying, dew-covered grass.

"We're still waiting, son. Mr. Morgan deserves to know why you think he's the one you saw."

Cliff looked up and made eye contact with everyone. "Okay, fine. From the size of the man, he was as tall as you, Mr. Morgan."

"How do you know?" The giant still sat facing Cliff, his hands cupping the edge of the porch, more relaxed now. "What did you use to compare his size with?"

"He had to duck under branches on trees that were at least six feet from the ground. We have the same kind of trees behind our house. He was carrying a full-grown pig, too."

The deputy shifted his weight from one foot to the other. "How do you know it was a full-grown pig?"

"From the squeal it made. It wasn't a young pig."

"Tell me about the man. What makes you think it was me? Never mind about his size."

"It *was* you...except..." Cliff squinted his eyes as he looked at Mr. Morgan.

Deputy Collins looked from Cliff to the giant and back. "Except what?"

"Well...I'm...I'm trying to see you before you cleaned up, cut your hair and shaved."

The giant grinned, showing straight, white teeth and looked back at Granny. Her belly shook, but she didn't make a sound as she laughed, the smile on her face radiant.

"Son, I haven't had long hair since the Army barber cut it before I went overseas to fight in the war." Then the big man stood, turned his back to the group, and took off his floppy hat, rubbing his close-cropped hair before turning back around. "I like my military haircut."

His jovial laughter was infectious on all but Cliff. "What's so funny?" He turned a reddened face toward Abraham first, then Hank, and stared at Daniel until his cousin choked on his own laughter, coughing violently. Hank slapped his back several times.

"I'm...all right.... Sorry Cliff...I couldn't...help...myself."

The older cousin stepped toward the giant, but the deputy sobered and took hold of his arm and held him back. "Not smart, young man. Get control of yourself."

"I don't like being laughed at."

The big man sat down again. "Son, no one is laughing at you. I'm sorry if we gave you that impression. I'm just glad to know the description you gave is definitely not mine at all."

"Why not?"

"What I'm about to tell you only a few people around here know. I do not shave because I cannot grow a beard. I am a full-blooded Indian, a Choctaw and Comanche half-breed."

"But..."

"It's okay. I'm used to people drawing conclusions about me that are wrong. I should be. I've dealt with it all my life. Believe me, this is not the first time, nor will it be the last time, people have misjudged me."

The deputy put a hand on Cliff's shoulder. "You see, son, if your father and his friend had been able to describe the person you had seen like you just did, we could have prevented the bounty from being put on our friend, Mr. Morgan. It was an honest mistake, but it could have cost this man his life because of the stir it has caused. I'm just glad it didn't come to that. And by the way, the sheriff and I are tracking down another lead that will clear Jeffrey, too. We just decided to have all the facts on the table before we made our suspicions public knowledge. Emotions are high enough without adding more speculation. The most dangerous situation is one out of control because of misinformation."

"Well, if we didn't see him, then who?" Cliff glanced at the giant before crossing his arms over his chest, again. "Who or what did we see? What about the prints we saw out near the river when we went to Spoon Bend?"

"Uh-oh." Daniel's blurted response and the deputy's sudden piercing look caused Hank's nerves to ignite the blood in his cheeks.

Mr. Pete returned his attention to Cliff. "I honestly don't know, but that isn't for you to worry about. The sheriff and I will take care of it. The main thing, right now, is for you to decide whether you are done with making these accusations that clearly slander Mr. Morgan's good name." He waited for Cliff to nod. "Good man. I think you need to apologize to Jeffrey and be grateful he doesn't hold it against you."

"Yes, sir. I'm sorry, Jeff…" The deputy cleared his throat. "Uh… Mr. Morgan."

Jeffrey remained seated, nodding with a wide grin on his face. "Forgiven, young man, but I don't want your handshake unless you mean it."

Cliff didn't move. Hank noticed his facial features soften when his resolve changed; and he reached for the big man's hand, pumping it when it was accepted.

"You have a strong handshake, young man. I am proud to call you my friend." Cliff grinned as Mr. Morgan shook with one hand and patted his back with the other.

"Thank you, sir. Me, too."

The giant stood, towering over everyone. "Now, how about we stop wasting time and get to work so this lovely woman and her young apprentice can do what they need to do, too."

Hank felt the deputy's stare before he looked up at him. The scowl on the man's face made his heart ache, and hot blood flooded his cheeks. *I feel like I've let you down, Daddy. It's not just about what you did, son, but what you're going to do now.* His eyes burned as he considered the truth of the words from his father's teachings. He moved toward Mr. Pete before the man had a chance to take a single step from where he stood. The closer he got, the more he realized Deputy Collins' eyes expressed fear rather than anger. "I'm sorry I didn't tell you about the tracking we did while at Spoon Bend. Until I heard Mr. Morgan say he wasn't in the area, I was afraid it was his camp Cliff had found. I should have told you."

The deputy's scowl softened before he gave Hank a bone-crushing bear hug. "Don't you know how much danger you were in out there? If anything had happened to you, son, I don't..."

Hank felt the man's body convulse. Suddenly, his mind returned to a day long ago, when he had been missing and his daddy had found him sleeping in the hayloft. It had been a few days before his fifth birthday and a couple of weeks before Daddy had left for the war. If he hadn't known better, Hank would have thought he was back in time and experiencing that same hug from his daddy now. Unshed tears stung his eyes. "I'm so sorry. It won't happen again, I promise."

Mr. Pete held Hank at arm's length without letting him go, yet. The grip more gentle, but still tight. Tears trailed down both the man's cheeks, staining his clean uniform shirt with wet spots. "Please don't. I can't protect you if I don't know where you are or what you're doing. I'm not trying to invade your privacy or keep you from standing on your own. It's just that you have to be smart about the adventures you take on your own. I love you too much to let you get hurt or let you hurt your family."

Hank swallowed back tears pooling in his eyes, near to overflowing. "I won't let you down again, Da..." An electric shock stabbed through all his nerves as he realized what he had almost called the deputy.

"You haven't let me down, son. I just want you to realize I see a lot of stuff I wish didn't exist. I would rather you not have to see that side of humanity any more than you have already."

"Yes, sir."

"Okay, let's put that behind us. The more important thing is what you decide to do now." He let out a long sigh. "What do you say we join the others and get on with this day?"

Hank smiled. *Just like you used to say, Daddy.* "Yes, sir." The deputy released his arms, and they turned to walk to the porch where everyone else gathered. "Wait." They paused in their trek to the others. "You're not going to tell Ma, are you? I mean…"

"Come on." The deputy put his arm around Hank's shoulders and pulled him along. "As long as you keep your word about not putting yourself in danger like that again, we're done here with the whole issue."

Hank looked up at him again, squinting from the brightness of the sun. "Is that like keeping secrets from her, though?"

Mr. Pete smiled. "No. It's keeping police business at the office and not taking it home, son."

"Oh. I guess that makes sense."

* * * * * * *

Everyone was in the watermelon patch today except Beth Ann and Granny. It was Hank's turn to drive the wagon while the other boys and Mr. Morgan filled it with their third load this morning. A few had burst open when they were set on the pile. The smell of sweet juice from the firm, red meat of the melons filled the air around the wagon. The memory of tasting a slice from the early crop of Granny's specially grown watermelons at the Fourth of July picnic made his mouth water. *These will taste even sweeter since they're from the later crop.* It was hard to keep from taking a break to eat a chunk before getting them back to the house. Hank shaded his eyes with his hand, estimating the time by the sun's position. *Almost noon.* Rumblings in his stomach made the smell of the burst melons even more inviting.

Mr. Morgan didn't have to look up at all to see Hank eye to eye. "Take us back to the barn, Mr. Baker. We're hungrier than a herd of buffalo on the prairie. How about you?"

"Yes, sir. Are you all riding or walking?"

The giant looked to the group putting the last of the watermelons for this load on the wagon. "What do you say, men? Are we riding or walking?"

Abraham took off his hat and wiped his face with his shirtsleeve. "If I ride, I might not want to do anything else the rest of the day. I'll walk."

Cliff patted the pile of melons. "Granny sure knows how to grow a good crop of melons, doesn't she? How many trips to the barn does this make now, three?"

Daniel huffed and puffed after lifting the last picked watermelon for this load onto the wagon. "Yeah, and they taste better than any I've had from anywhere else, too. How many more loads do you think are left, Mr. Morgan?"

The big man looked at the rest of the field before wiping his face with a red rag he kept in the back pocket of his overalls. "Oh, at least one more, maybe two."

Cliff climbed up to sit beside Hank. "What will she do with all these melons?"

Abraham grabbed the harness on the mule on the left, removing the feed bag and rubbing its nose, then he did the same for the other mule. "Lots of people buy Granny's melons from as far away as Hope."

Hank whistled and snapped the reins. "She also donates all the melons for the church picnics and the socials that go on during the annual tent revival meetings."

The group quieted down as they made their way to the barn from the field at the back of Granny's property. Hank went no faster than the three walking. That way, they all arrived together.

When they came around the last bend, Hank pulled on the reins and stopped the mules without warning anyone. He stood and pointed toward the house.

"Look, isn't that the preacher's wagon and team?" His heart began to beat hard against his ribcage. He scratched the back of his neck, then looked at his hand and back at the house. "Oh, no. The sheriff's here, too. Something's wrong."

CHAPTER 13

N° ONE MOVED AS THEY watched the sheriff park his motor car beside Pastor Bob's buckboard. When he got out of the car, he draped his arms over the top of the door for several seconds before closing it and looked around until he saw the group. *It's not good news.* He waved them to come on in, and then he waited in front of his car with his feet shoulder-width apart and his fists on his hips. Hank tried to swallow the lump in his throat. He couldn't tell if the look on Sheriff Stan's face was worry or a reaction to the bright sunshine and heat.

"He's here on business, and it looks to be serious. I told you something was wrong." He looked at Cliff's profile, his mind volleying between anger at the trouble Daniel's cousin has caused and fear that the sheriff was bringing bad news about Mr. Pete. *After all, why else would he be at Granny's?*

"Are you ever wrong about those feelings?"

Hank looked from Cliff to the man waiting for them. "Not yet."

Mr. Morgan slapped one of the mules on the rump, prodding it to pull the wagon forward again. "Don't borrow trouble that may not come, son. You kids take this load of melons to the barn. We'll unload them after we have something to eat. Go ahead and unhitch Samson and Delilah from the wagon and put the feed sacks back on them, then come on up to the house. I'll see why the sheriff's here."

Hank knew he didn't have to drive the mules to the barn because they knew the way. Instead, he kept a close watch on the sheriff and Mr. Morgan. They shook hands, smiled, and then talked in hushed tones as the wagon passed them on the way to the barn. Sheriff Stan put a foot on the bumper of his motor car and clasped his hands together, draping one arm over his raised leg. *Looks friendly enough. Neither of them appears to be upset about anything. That's good, isn't it?*

Hank rubbed the back of his neck again and looked back at the men. *There's still something wrong, though.* He saw the giant rub his chin, looking at the ground under his feet then at the sheriff's face. Mr. Morgan nodded as he crossed his arms over his chest. Then both men laughed. Hank relaxed a little bit, but couldn't shake the feeling of impending trouble. He looked around the farm, his eyes drawn to the pen where Buster was kept. *Buster? No, I don't think...* Then his focus shifted to the woods toward the back of Granny's property. Just beyond it was the Baker property.

Before he could assess the possible connection between the woods and his gut instincts, Abraham and Daniel led Samson and Delilah inside the barn. The pungent odors from the stalls, mixed with the sweet smell of the split watermelons assaulted Hank's senses, snapping him back to the task at hand; but he remained on alert, the tension from outside still haunting his subconscious thoughts.

Cliff jumped down from his seat next to Hank. "What should we do with the busted melons?"

Daniel grabbed the feed bags while Abraham unhitched the mules from the wagon. "Maybe Granny will let us eat them when we're finished later today, if not for dessert." He sniffed, then coughed, fanning his nose. "Whew! They smell good, but not enough to cover the other smells in here. I say we take them to the house so they don't spoil from the exposure to this place."

Abraham took the bags from Daniel. "I'm hungry enough to eat one by myself."

"I hear that. Wait till you taste one of Granny's melons, Cliff. You won't eat another one without comparing it to hers." Daniel smacked his lips. "I wonder why the preacher is here. Did you know he was coming by, Abraham?"

"No, but the tent revival is coming up in a week or so. Maybe he's here about that."

Hank stood back from the others while they carefully lifted the burst melons from the pile on the wagon. "I'm telling you, something's not right."

Daniel shifted the melon he held and almost dropped it. "Whoa! Careful! Boy this one sure smells sweet. I can taste it now. M-m-m! There, now I've got it. If you think about it, when is anything *ever* right at Granny's?"

"Seriously, guys."

Abraham had a melon under each arm, juice dripping from the cracks in both of them. "Is that spot on your neck tingling, again? Is that why you're saying that?"

"Actually, yeah. What I can't figure is whether it's because of the preacher being here or the sheriff or something else."

Cliff handed Hank a melon. "Has anyone ever told you that you worry a lot? Here, take your mind off that stuff and carry this up to the house. But then again, maybe you have something there. I'm not totally convinced Mr. Morgan wasn't in the woods near Roark's Landing when we crossed the river. How do you know he's telling us the truth?"

He took the melon, careful to avoid the dripping juice. "Why are you so sure he isn't?" Anger and annoyance crowded Hank's heart.

"Look, I'm not trying to start anything. I'm just saying you're taking a big chance with this guy. I mean, where does he come from? He's not from around here, is he? Just how well do you really know him?"

Abraham waited for the others just outside the barn door. "All I need to know is what I see in him. If it weren't for him, my family and I wouldn't be here. He saved our lives. That makes him more than okay as far as I'm concerned. He didn't have to know anything about me to risk his own life for mine. You could learn a lot from him, like how to trust people more than you do. Now, are we going to stand around here talking or get on up to the house so we can have some of this watermelon that's making my stomach rumble every time I smell it?"

Daniel smacked his lips again, leaving everyone else behind, practically running toward the house. "I'm not talking. I'm ready to eat."

* * * * * * *

Mr. Morgan was already at the water pump in the backyard. "Take those melons to the back porch, boys. Then come get cleaned up. The preachers are joining us for lunch. Granny and Beth Ann have fixed a feast in there for us all. So hurry up. It smells really good all the way out here. Let's not keep them waiting."

Hank stayed behind the others. "Preachers?"

"Yeah, the circuit preacher is with the pastor."

"But the revival isn't for another week and a half."

"He's making the rounds visiting folks, inviting them to the meetings, and getting acquainted, I guess. Go on, now. Get that melon put on the table on the back porch."

"Yes, sir." He took a couple of steps toward the house, then returned to the pump. "Is the sheriff staying, too?"

"No, he had to leave. Duty calls, and all, you know."

"Yes, sir." He took several steps then returned. "Is everything all right? I mean, you aren't in trouble, are you? Mr. Pete is okay?"

Mr. Morgan dried his hands and arms on a towel he had tucked in his back pocket. He shook his head, smiling. "You worry a lot, don't you? Everything's just fine, my young friend. Your Mr. Pete is, too. Now, go. The others are coming to wash up. The food is waiting. Aren't you hungry?"

Hank grinned, even though his heart still carried a burden. "Yes, sir."

* * * * * * *

Granny and Beth Ann had outdone themselves with the meal. There was pan-fried chicken, mashed potatoes, gravy, fresh corn-on-the-cob, lima beans, cornbread, and apple cobbler for dessert. Laughter and friendly chatter filled the kitchen as the diners ate and enjoyed the feast laid before them.

Hank sized up the circuit preacher, ignoring the conversation around the table. He was a big man, tall, balding, and hefty. His high cheekbones and easy smile added a perpetual cheerfulness and friendliness to his disposition. *A body can't help but be drawn to him.* Hank squirmed when he noticed the man's perusal of him, which seemed to be almost constant. *I wish he'd stop that. It's making me nervous.* He studied Reverend Adams as he chewed, taking more time than usual to chew between bites. Hank saw the similarity of his skin color with Mr. Morgan's; but the circuit preacher's blue eyes and thick mustache and beard canceled any obvious Indian heritage.

"Well, Mrs. Massey..."

"Call me 'Granny,' reverend. Everybody does around these parts."

Reverend Adams' belly shook as he chuckled. "All right, then. Granny, that was a marvelous meal. Miss Beth Ann, you are an excellent helper for this fine lady. I have to say your apple cobbler has to be from a blue-ribbon recipe. If I'm not careful, I'll gain another inch or two around my middle before this tent revival is over."

Everyone laughed, except Hank. He grinned, but the feeling of something wrong wouldn't let go. He had resisted rubbing the back of his neck throughout the meal.

"You're welcome to come again, anytime, both of you."

129

"While I'm at it, let me thank you again for allowing us to raise the tent on your property for the duration of the meetings. I truly think the attendance will be such that the space you have here is going to be necessary. The church lot is too small for the crowds I believe will come. And Abraham, I hope you'll join us as often as you can."

"Thank you, sir; but I'll be attending services at the camp meeting happening at the same time at Beech Hill where my family lives."

"Well, that's fine." The circuit preacher stood. "Bob, my friend, we have a few more stops to make before dark. If they're as good as this one, we may not get to them all today. Shall we go?"

The pastor wiped his mouth and stood. "Thank you, folks, for the company. It was a pleasure to see you all and it not be a Sunday." Everyone laughed again. "Beth Ann, your daddy and mama are so proud of you helping out around here, learning from this sweet lady. Granny, you are the perfect hostess, as usual. The meal was the best I've had all week. Take care, now. We'll see ourselves out. You boys don't work too hard this afternoon, now. Drink lots of water. It's going to be another hot one."

Everyone stood as the two preachers made their way to the front door. Hank watched Mr. Morgan hug Granny and kiss her cheek. "Good meal, Aunt Rosie, thanks."

Aunt Rosie? Could that be why he comes over here so much? I wonder. Hank paid close attention to the interaction between the two.

The big man had to bow his back to lean against the ladder back chair in front of him. "You know, you have some good workers here. They have a really good work rhythm as a team. We'll be done before you know it today. Ready, boys? We can call it a day after we take care of that last load of melons in the field. But we can't do that until we unload the wagon in the barn. Let's get it done."

"You ought to know by now that I don't hire slackers. To show my gratitude for the diligent work you all are doing, I'll get those busted melons on the porch ready so you can have some before you go home."

Daniel's grin was all teeth. "Yes, ma'am! Come on, guys. My mouth is watering already."

Hank laughed in spite of his mood. *Daniel, I think she's winning you over without you realizing it.*

"Jeffrey, would you take some scraps to Buster? He didn't look so good this morning. Maybe some gravy and meat will make him feel better. I don't think he likes being cooped up."

"Sure. How much longer will he need to be in the pen?"

"Another week, at least."

"I'll give this to him."

"I'll go with him, Granny." Hank tossed his napkin next to his empty plate.

"You don't get too close. Don't even pet him. If he has rabies, you could get infected. Just because he hasn't shown signs yet, it doesn't mean he doesn't have it."

"Yes, ma'am."

The dog pen was between the house and the barn, but not close to any other structures. The other boys were already at the barn when they reached the pen. Buster raised his head, but lowered it again, showing no interest in the table scraps at all.

"That's not a good sign, is it?"

"No, son. It isn't." The big man sighed. "Time's wasting. We need to get back to work." He set the plate just inside the pen, testing the chain that locked the gate.

"Yes, sir."

By mid-afternoon, the last of the watermelons was put on the wagon. Daniel and Cliff kept a steady stream of stories from family reunions going as they worked, keeping everyone entertained. Hank realized the feelings of something wrong were gone when he couldn't stop himself from laughing so hard he had tears in his eyes. He was glad because it felt good to laugh. It also made the work go faster. It only took a couple of hours to finish harvesting the watermelons. Cliff was a different person, too. For the first time since being around him, Hank felt Daniel's cousin was completely relaxed and himself for a change.

Beth Ann and Granny joined the five field hands on the porch for the reddest, sweetest, juiciest watermelon in Ouachita and Union Counties, possibly the whole state. Hank enjoyed himself so much, he forgot to be concerned about his earlier feelings. Even Cliff continued to be pleasant company.

Daniel rubbed his belly. "Granny, that was the best watermelon I've had all summer. How do you do it? Actually, I think they get better every year."

She smiled, gathering the forks. "I'm glad you enjoyed that, honey. There's nothing I like more than knowing you appreciate what's given to you. Will you please take the rinds to the chicken yard. Use the bucket there if you want." She went inside while they deposited their own rinds in the bucket.

Cliff grinned. "She definitely has the magic touch for growing the best watermelons I've tasted."

Daniel's smile became of frown instantly, and he gulped. "Seriously?"

Beth Ann rolled her eyes. "Oh, brother! Now you've done it. Thanks a lot. Just when I thought he'd gotten past all that, you go and stir up his superstitions again."

Hank put his arm around his best friend. "Now, Daniel, you know everybody says Granny has a green thumb when it comes to crops. She's not a witch."

Cliff held the screen door open for everyone, still grinning. "There's an easy way to settle that. Did you swallow a seed while you were enjoying the fruit of her labor, cousin?"

Daniel's eyes looked like they would pop out if he sneezed. "Yeah. A couple, maybe. Why?"

His cousin chuckled. "Well, there you have it. That's the test. If you swallow a watermelon seed, but a melon doesn't grow in your belly, she's not a witch. Ow, girl! Why'd you do that?" Cliff rubbed his upper arm, frowning at the sight of a small raised knot that had appeared.

Beth Ann started to punch him again in the stomach, but Hank grabbed her fist. "Don't mind him. It's not worth the effort."

"Don't listen to him, Daniel. You'll be fine."

Cliff laughed harder. "Watch out for the swelling in your belly, cousin."

Hank and Abraham snickered, but sobered when Daniel set his rinds down and looked at his stomach, using both hands to measure the size of his full belly.

"Cliff, you're mean, you hear me? Mean to the bone. Come on, Daniel." Beth Ann gave him the look Hank saw on his mother's face more than a few times.

"Boy, Abraham, does she have that look down pat, or what?"

"Scary, isn't it?" His teeth were bright against his dark skin.

"Yeah, we'd better get these to the chicken yard. Mr. Pete will be here any minute, now."

Cliff laughed louder with every step he took. Neither Hank nor Abraham could help themselves. It was an infectious laugh that could not be stopped. Before long, Beth Ann and Daniel were laughing, too.

* * * * * * *

Hank was grateful for Mr. Pete's help with the evening chores. He had difficulty staying awake through dinner. When he awoke in the middle of the night with a start, he barely remembered climbing into bed. The clock in the front room chimed eleven times. *Why am I awake?* Then he heard it—the woman's scream, coming from the Milner farm.

133

CHAPTER 14

*T*HAT WASN'T MY IMAGINATION OR *a dream.* He quickly got out of bed and noticed his brother's bed was empty. His heart skipped a couple of beats. *Where's Jimmy Jack? God, where's my brother?* He raced to the window, leaning way out to get a better view of the yard and property. Nothing appeared out of the ordinary and all was quiet on the Baker farm. Then he heard the door of the outhouse shut with a sharp snap. *If that's you, Jimmy Jack, hurry. Get back in the house quick.*

He hurried to the door to open it when he heard running footsteps in the hall coming closer to the room. As he stepped through the door, his brother ran into him, nearly knocking him down.

"Jimmy Jack! Shhh! Don't wake up Ma."

"Did you hear that?"

"Yeah."

"What was it? It sounded like somebody screaming."

"I think it was the cat."

"The one that was here yesterday morning?"

"Maybe. Mr. Pete said panthers can sound like a woman screaming sometimes."

"Boys?" Ma stood in the doorway.

"Ahhhh!" Hank's toes grew roots into the floor, but his knees threatened to buckle on him. Jimmy jumped onto his bed and covered up so only his eyes were visible.

"Boys! What on earth is going on?"

Hank blurted out everything way too fast, every nerve on edge. "Jimmy Jack wasn't in his bed when I woke up just now, and I was worried, and he had gone to the outhouse but came running in when the cat screamed, and Ma, you just scared me half to death."

"Hank! Stop. Breathe." Ma sat on Jimmy's bed and took the sheet off his face. "Now slow down and start over."

"Something woke me. I was just about to go back to sleep when I heard the cat scream from the direction of the Milners' farm. When I got up to look out the window, I noticed Jimmy wasn't in bed. I didn't see him outside, but I heard the outhouse door slam. So I decided to go looking for him, but he came barreling down the hallway and nearly knocked me down. Then you..."

Just then, the cat screamed again; and Jimmy pulled the sheet back over his head. Hank and Ma went to the window at the same time. They leaned out, side by side, craning to see the Milners' farm.

"That was farther away this time."

"Okay, I want you boys to stay inside the house."

"I'm not going anywhere." The muffled voice broke the tension. The more Hank tried not to laugh, the more powerful the need to let it go became. He collapsed on top of his covers and giggled so hard his sides hurt and tears streamed down his face. When he sat up and found Ma and Jimmy sitting together and laughing just as hard, he succumbed to another fit of uncontrollable laughter.

"Okay." Ma gained control first. "That's enough." She wiped her eyes with the back of her hands. "I just hope nothing happened to any of Mr. Milner's cows. There's really nothing we can do at this hour. It's going on midnight; and you have to get up early again tomorrow, Hank. Go on back to bed. We'll tell Pete what we heard when he gets here in the morning. Until then, please don't go outside."

Suddenly, a light shone through the front windows.

"Someone's here, Ma."

"Just stay put. I'll see who it is." She padded to the front room.

Hank lit the lamp on the nightstand, his heart still pounding. The sound of a frantic knock distracted him till the match burned his fingers. He violently shook the flame out. He could distinguish a male voice from Ma's, but it was too garbled to identify positively.

"Mr. Pete!" Jimmy jumped out of bed.

"Wait. Don't you leave this room." Hank grabbed him by the collar of his nightshirt. "Just wait." They both leaned out of the room as far as they dared, craning their necks to see who had arrived.

When they heard the door close and Ma coming toward them, they scooted back into the bedroom and to their beds, ready to go to sleep again when she looked in on them.

"That was Pete. He heard the screams, too, and thought they were coming from here. He's going to check out the Milner farm next." She sighed. "Now, go back to bed, both of you, and get some sleep." She tucked Jimmy back in bed and kissed him on the cheek. Then she sat on Hank's bed. "Please be careful when you're out there, even in the daylight. Don't take any chances." She smoothed back the hair that had fallen over his brow. "You need a haircut, young man."

"Yes, ma'am."

"You look so much like your father, son." She kissed the top of his head. "You make us so proud, your daddy and me, how you've grown and how you take care of your brother and the farm. I wish he could see you. Maybe he can. Maybe God lets him look in on us every now and then. Get some sleep, now. Tomorrow's going to be another busy day for you."

"Yes, ma'am."

137

"Good night, son. I love you."

"Good night." She was about to close the door. "Ma?"

She looked around the door at him. "Yeah?"

"What do you think Daddy would say about Mr. Pete?"

She thought a moment. "I think he'd be happy to know there's someone who cares about us and loves us as much as he did. Why do you ask?"

He paused. "Just wondering. I love you, Ma."

"Go to sleep, now."

"Yes, ma'am." He turned to face the wall. *How can I be sure that's how you'd feel, Daddy?*

* * * * * * *

As he completed each chore, Hank searched for signs of the cat, but there were no new tracks. *Whew! Thank you, God. I just hope nothing happened at the Milners' last night.* Just as he and Jimmy finished their work, Mr. Pete drove up. Hank watched his little brother run and jump into the deputy's arms. When he put the boy down, he waved to Hank who waved back. Breakfast was on the table when they all three entered the kitchen.

"Smells good. I've had a long night, and I'm starved." Deputy Collins kissed Ma before sitting down.

"What did you find out at the Milners'?" Ma poured a third glass of milk before putting the pitcher back into the icebox.

"He lost a heifer."

"Oh, no."

"Mr. Pete, was it the cat that got the heifer?" Hank held his breath.

The deputy nodded. "Yep. There were tracks all around his place, just like my drawings."

"What happens now?" Martha sat in the chair between Pete and Jimmy.

"The sheriff is getting a group of men together this morning to hunt the panther, hoping to get it before nightfall. With clear evidence of a cat, maybe people will come to their senses and stop making Jeffrey the scapegoat for what Stan and I always thought was killing the livestock. Without proof, no one wanted to hear it."

"Can I go on the hunt with you?" Excitement built in Hank's mind, eager to tell Cliff how wrong he'd been to accuse Mr. Morgan.

"Absolutely not!" Ma's face was pale, her eyes blazing with terror.

Pete covered her hand with his. "I'd rather you stay with the others at Granny's. She and Beth Ann need someone with a level head watching out for them. Between you and Abraham, they'll be safe, even if the cat were to come onto her property. I trust you two to handle yourselves with a gun responsibly and keep Granny from doing anything that will get her hurt. And before you think otherwise, I'm not saying I don't trust Daniel or Cliff. But I *know* you and Abraham and what you're capable of in a crisis. I need you more at Granny's than in the woods today."

"Yes, sir."

"As a matter of fact, I'm going to suggest you not go back to harvesting Granny's crops until we have eliminated this danger."

"Will you kill it?"

"It's a killer, son. It's the only way to insure safety. As it is, it has lost its fear of humans, to a degree. It's not afraid to hunt in areas where the human scent is prominent. It's just a matter of time before it starts hunting people. We won't let that happen."

"I'll bet the Golden Eagle could stop it." Jimmy took a bite of bacon.

"The Golden Eagle?" The deputy looked from the boy to Hank, his brows furrowed.

"Yeah. He's really fast and strong. My friends have seen him. He can break a tree limb without using his leg, and he can climb a tree faster than they've ever seen."

Pete looked at Martha and smiled. "Is that so?"

"Yep." Jimmy shoveled his eggs into his mouth, a drip of bright yellow yolk on his chin. He used the back of his hand to wipe it, then licked it off his hand.

"Well, that's something. Do you know who this Golden Eagle is? Maybe I could talk with him and get his take on all of this."

Jimmy wiped his face and hands on his napkin. "I'll ask around if you want. As far as I know, no one knows who he is. He wears a mask and cape."

"Are you sure he isn't a criminal that Sheriff Stan and I need to investigate?"

The boy's head jerked to look at the deputy with wide eyes. "No, sir! He's a good guy. He's not a criminal."

"Wow! Your loyalty to him is very impressive. Are you sure you don't know who he is?" Hank grinned at the banter.

"I just know he's a good guy. You don't have to worry about him."

Ma stood and gathered the dirty dishes from the table. "Well, that settles that. How about you let Pete and Hank finish their breakfast so they don't waste any more of the morning?"

"Aw, Ma."

"Your ma's right, son. I still need to pick up the others and get them to Granny's. Are you ready, Hank?"

He finished his milk, wiping the white mustache from the corners of his mouth with his napkin. "Yes, sir."

"Me, too."

* * * * * * *

When the deputy arrived at Granny's, there were only three hands instead of four. Cliff joined the hunt with his father and their friend. Before any of them could get out of the car, Granny ran across the back yard to the hen house with a hoe in her hands.

Daniel looked up at the deputy. "Wow! She's faster than I thought she'd be. Look at her run; but what's she doing, deputy?"

140

He grinned. "Snake. That woman hates snakes worse than trespassers. Hurry and get out. Run around to the back so you can see what she found."

They all scrambled to get around to the back yard. They were winded, but stood agog when she emerged from the hen house with a long black snake draped around the end of the hoe. Raw eggs dripped from its lifeless mouth.

"Whoa! He's at least four feet long." Daniel's mouth hung open.

Hank reached over and closed it. "Flies. Better close your mouth so you don't attract flies."

The deputy grunted. "That's a small one. Doesn't matter, though. If it's a snake, she's going to kill it. I wonder how many eggs he ate before she got him?"

Beth Ann scrunched her nose. "Nasty. Looks like more than a few."

Daniel snickered. "How is it you see blood and broken bones and stuff without any kind of reaction, but you get squeamish at a snake draining eggs out of its mouth?"

She put her hand over her stomach. "Shut up."

"Why didn't she just let Abraham get it, Mr. Pete."

"Hank, that sweet, kind, gentle woman has declared war on all kinds of snakes. She goes after them with a vengeance. For some reason, unknown to me, she gets a distinct pleasure out of killing them. Maybe it's her way of avenging Adam. Come on, time to let her know you're here." The deputy strode toward the hen house.

Daniel furrowed his brows. "Adam who?"

Beth Ann laughed. "You really don't know? Adam—from the Garden of Eden?"

"What did snakes do to him?"

"Oh, brother. You really need to be paying closer attention in church instead of worrying about Granny and her *evil eye*." She ran to catch up to the deputy.

"Hank, do you know what she's talking about?"

He laughed and followed the others. He stayed behind a moment then ran after them. "Oh! Eve, the...uh...apple? The serpent, in the Garden of Eden. I get it now. Wait up!"

* * * * * * *

With Cliff helping the sheriff hunt the cat, Abraham, Daniel, and Hank were left to do outhouse duty, digging the new hole then filling in the old one. When that was done, Granny wanted them to dig three more holes out near where the tent for the revival meetings was staked out. They decided to work together on Granny's, and then they would each dig a hole for the others, making as quick work of it as they could. Their job was digging. Mr. Morgan and Mr. Pete would do the building of the structures once the holes were ready.

It was Hank's turn to dig while Abraham and Daniel rested a bit. "So the cat got Sadie, too? Why didn't Eddie report it to the sheriff?"

Abraham wiped his face with the red rag he kept in the back pocket of his overalls. "The deputy said he was scared. He couldn't blame the cat for taking Sadie. Everybody in town was talking about her being stolen in broad daylight."

Daniel plucked a piece of grass and put it in his mouth. "Yeah, Eddie Phillips is a bad liar anyway. That's why he always gets caught. I'm not surprised he's a bootlegger, but where he had his still does surprise me. Setting it up on Granny's property was the dumbest thing he could have done. Why put it here?"

"According to what he told the sheriff, he knew no G-man would look on her property because of who she is. When Mr. Morgan came upon it, he smashed it up. What he didn't know was Eddie saw him do it. So he followed him to Granny's and assumed she had told him to bust it up. He took Sadie to get even with her."

"Now, that was worse than dumb." Hank rested his arm across the top of the shovel handle, looking up at the other two. "What did he do, panic when he found Sadie's dead carcass?"

Abraham chuckled. "The deputy said he couldn't tell his side fast enough. He said he wanted protection from Granny because he was afraid she'd stake him out with rawhide and leave him for dead when she found out. Personally, I think he's read too many dime novel stories about Indians. It wasn't till he heard about the cat that killed Mr. Milner's heifer that he told the sheriff about the cat tracks around Sadie's carcass."

Daniel laughed. "Goes to show you how gullible criminals can be, believing the worst about good people."

Hank stopped again and stared at his best friend, joining the laughter. "Down right ironic, isn't it." He winked at Abraham.

Suddenly, Daniel sobered. "What was that for? Why'd you wink at him?"

Hank grinned as he got back to digging. "Must have got some dirt in my eye. Your turn in the hole, Daniel."

As he climbed out of the hole, Daniel was about to jump in, until Hank and Abraham turned at the sound of the screen door slamming and saw Beth Ann running toward them.

Hank's furrowed brows deepened the closer she got. "Wait, Daniel. Something's happened."

CHAPTER 15

BETH ANN STOPPED WITHIN A couple of feet of the boys. "I was taking Buster some food when I noticed he was acting funny. Granny wants you to check on him, Abraham. I think he's got rabies."

They looked at one another. Abraham's skin looked a shade lighter to Hank. "Come on, let's check it out." As they drew near the pen, he spread his arms out, preventing Daniel and Beth Ann from getting any closer. "I've never seen rabies, Abraham. Have you?"

White foam bubbled around the dog's mouth. He snarled and snapped his teeth, his shaking head slinging drool on his fur and on the ground.

The colored boy wiped sweat from his mouth and brow with his sleeve before putting his hands on his hips, one foot slightly in front of the other. He had filled his cheeks with air, blowing it out in a huff. "Yeah. It looks just like that." He nodded toward the pen. "The animal is in so much pain, it thinks everything and everyone is a threat."

Daniel sucked in air. "What about Granny? Didn't she treat his wounds?"

"Yeah, but she used some kind of medicine she put together and washed with lye soap every few minutes while she cleaned him up. It's something she said she learned from her grandfather or uncle or someone who was a medicine man. The deputy was concerned, but she said she'd used it before without getting sick. I guess it's a family secret. I just know she wouldn't let me or him near Buster while she worked on him."

Hank crossed his arms over his chest. "Why didn't she use the medicine on Buster?"

"That's what the deputy asked her. Since she didn't know how long he had been exposed, she couldn't be sure it would work on him. She was real careful not to get his blood on her or let him lick her. When she put him in the pen, she used a rope to pull him along. She let him take his time, but he had to walk out here on his own. He's been here ever since, almost three weeks. She wanted him…what's the word?"

Beth Ann wiped her eyes and sniffed. "Quarantined."

"That's it. She wanted him quarantined at least a month, just in case it took that long to show up."

Hank sighed. "I guess whatever medicine she used kept it from showing up till now. Doesn't it usually come on quicker?"

"Yeah."

Beth Ann's voice was shaky. "He's suffering, poor thing."

Daniel tossed a twig to the side and shook his head. "He has to be put down."

"Yeah, then we'll have to burn him with the pen so it doesn't spread." Abraham turned toward the house. "Wait here. I'll see what Granny wants to do."

He jogged on up to the house.

* * * * * * *

Hank's heart ached, watching Beth Ann cry as Granny hugged her. The smoke from the pen rose into the sky, the heat intense. The three boys surrounded the fire with buckets of water ready to contain it should a spark ignite the dry grass outside the water-filled trench around the pen. As the fire burned itself out, consuming the wood from the pen and the dead dog under it, the group was quiet.

Hank approached Granny and Beth Ann. "I'm so sorry about Buster, Granny. Are you sure you're okay? You aren't going to get sick, are you?"

She smiled and shook her head, squeezing Beth Ann's trembling shoulders. "No, son. I'm just fine. I've done this before. Don't you worry."

Hank nodded and returned to stand watch over the smoking embers.

Granny was somber. "Good job, Abraham. We're going back to the house now. It should be okay to leave it to burn itself out. Go on and wash up. We'll have some lunch before you get back to the outhouses."

"Yes, ma'am."

The boys gathered around the water pump. Hank pulled on the handle for the other two, then Daniel took over while he washed up. "I wonder how the hunt is going."

Hank shook the excess water from his hair. "Mr. Pete hoped it wouldn't take long." He took the towel Abraham offered to dry his hands. "Thanks. Do you know if Mr. Morgan went with them? I haven't seen him today."

"Come to think of it, I haven't seen him either. Knowing him, he probably got to the sheriff's office before the sheriff did."

Daniel washed his hands once more before the water stopped flowing and ran his fingers through his hair. "I wonder how he can be so quiet when he walks through the woods."

Hank tossed Daniel the towel. "Survival probably. Remember, he was in the Army and his being an Indian...."

"Maybe he'll teach us. It could come in handy when we're investigating stuff to be able to get around without anyone knowing we're anywhere near till it's too late."

Abraham shook his head and grinned.

"What?"

The colored boy shrugged his shoulders. "You are so practical, even with all your little quirks. That's what I like about you, Daniel. You're always thinking ahead, looking for ways to use what you learn to improve your God-given talents."

"Quirks? I have quirks? Like what?"

Hank laughed. "I've told you you're one in a million. God broke the mold when he made you. That's what I like about you most of all. There's only one Daniel Wagner."

"Yeah, well, you have to like me. We're practically twins."

Abraham furrowed his brows. "Twins?"

Daniel tossed the towel to Hank. "We were born on the same day just a few minutes apart, in the same hospital even, only we were in different rooms!"

"Seriously?" The colored boy raised his eyebrows toward his hairline. "That explains a lot."

Hank walked backwards. "I don't know about you two, but I'm ready to get some food, sustenance, lunch. Who's with me?" He turned and jogged to the house.

The other two passed him within seconds. The three raced for the screen door, nearly knocking Beth Ann down on the porch. "Hey, watch it. Where are your manners?" Her scowl softened as her grin spread.

"Sorry." They stood at attention, as if waiting for an inspection, trying to be sober; but a snicker escaped from them till they chuckled.

"Did you know I have quirks?"

She joined the laughter. "You're just now finding that out? We've been trying to tell you that for years. Come on. I was coming to get you. Lunch is on the table."

Daniel looked at the others, smiled, and then saluted her. "Yes, ma'am." The others did the same.

* * * * * * *

Hank and Abraham hugged Granny and kissed her cheek before getting back to work. "Thanks for lunch."

She patted each of them on the back. "You're welcome."

They waited for Daniel at the door, watching to see if he would follow their lead. He hesitated momentarily then gave her a brief squeeze and pecked her on the cheek, barely making contact with her skin. His face was red when he saw the others looking at him. Hank saw the twinkle in the woman's eyes when she watched him hurry out the door. Beth Ann grinned and shook her head. "He's growing up, Granny."

Hank giggled, proud of Daniel. "See you later, ladies. Let's go. You're after Daniel in the hole since I was the last one in before we were interrupted."

"Yep. See you later, Granny."

They met Daniel in the yard. "Do me a favor, guys. Don't tell Cliff what I just did. I can't believe I did it, either; but he'll just make a bigger deal out of it than it was."

"Like I've said before. You're one in a million, but I can't help but love you like a brother."

It took a little more than an hour to finish digging the hole, and the outhouse was properly placed. All that was left was filling in the old hole. They were nearly finished when the boys heard a motor car drive up to the house. A couple of minutes later, the deputy walked around the corner and waved.

"Oh, she had you digging the new hole, huh? I'm glad I was on duty."

Hank leaned against the handle of his shovel. "How's the hunt going?"

"No cat, yet, but we've found fresh tracks. I'm here to take you kids home, then get back. I need to check in with Granny, so you have time to finish up before we need to leave."

"Yes, sir." As Hank watched him go to the house, he scratched the tingle at the nape of his neck.

It only took another half-hour to finish filling the hole. They put the shovels away, washed up at the pump, and turned in time to see Beth Ann and the deputy walking toward them from the back porch. "Abraham." Deputy Collins shook his hand. "I truly appreciate you and all you do around here. Granny told me about Buster. Thank you so much for taking care of that for us."

"You're welcome, sir."

"As a matter of fact, we need to be on the lookout for other signs of rabies. We've come across a few dead carcasses that were obviously infected. Several of the men have been talking about killing varmints on their properties that were showing the signs. Don't take any chances if you see an animal behaving crazy or threatening your safety."

Beth Ann shaded her eyes with her hands cupped against her forehead. "Deputy, what about the cat? Do you think it's rabid?"

Hank shifted on his feet. "I was going to ask the same thing."

"I don't think so. The animals it's been eating weren't infected, and there's no sign of it being sick. It's just a rogue cat that's found an easy hunting ground. But we need to stop it before it does get infected and causes even more problems than it is now. Let's get you home so I can get back out there."

Daniel's eyes brightened. "Will there be anyone hunting through the night? I wouldn't mind Cliff staying out all night." He raised and lowered his eyebrows a couple of times, smiling.

The deputy chuckled. "He's not that bad, is he?" He ruffled the boy's hair. "To answer your question, there will be a few of us watching the farms around the area, just in case it decides to hunt for another easy meal. I don't know if Cliff and his father and friend have volunteered."

"I hope they did. He's really getting on my nerves. Ma keeps saying she's on her last nerve with him, too."

Everyone snickered. "Come on, now. I need to get you kids home. See you in the morning, Abraham."

"Yes, sir. See you guys tomorrow, too."

* * * * * * *

The drive home was quiet with only Hank and Mr. Pete in the motor car. "What's on your mind, son?"

"I was just thinking about a dream I had the other night."

"Care to share? It might help."

Hank looked at him. "It was about Mr. Morgan, you, and Daddy. I just can't figure out what it means. Do you think dreams have meanings?"

"Sometimes, but they don't have to be anything more than just your mind still playing while you sleep."

He nodded. "Lately, my dreams seem to mean something; but I don't know what this one is trying to tell me."

"Tell me about it."

"Mr. Morgan, you, and Daddy are sitting around a campfire. It looks like you're camping somewhere around Frenchport Landing. You're all like old friends, talking and laughing until the noise from an animal fight draws your attention to the woods behind you. Before you can do anything, a large, tall man with long, matted hair, wearing rags and a beard attacks you. He kind of reminds me of the description Cliff gave of the man they saw near Roark's Landing. He acts crazy-like. Do you think he could have been infected with rabies?"

"I don't know, maybe. What happened next?"

"Well, he starts screaming like a banshee, so you all grab your weapons; but Mr. Morgan's rifle misfires. You shoot just before the mad man grabs my daddy in a bear hug, then he falls on top of him. Daddy can't fire his pistol, and then everything gets quiet again. When Mr. Morgan rolls the man off him, they're both dead. That's when I wake up."

The deputy whistled. "That quite a dream. How often have you had it?"

"Just once, but I can't get it out of my head."

"No ideas about what it could mean?"

Hank shook his head. "Not a clue."

"Does it *have* to mean anything?"

"I guess not; but if it's not important, why can't I get it out of my mind?"

The deputy turned into the drive and parked under the sweet gum tree near the front yard. "You've had a lot on your mind lately—the livestock killings, the bounty on Mr. Morgan, and my asking you about marrying your ma. Maybe that's why you had the dream. It seems to me there are elements represented from each of the situations we're dealing with right now."

"I didn't think about that."

Just then, headlights shone from the end of the driveway leading to the Baker house. "Looks like you have company coming." They watched Beth Ann's father's car pull up beside the deputy. "Oh, it's Dr. Warden and Pastor Bob with the circuit preacher. What's his name—Calvin something."

"Adams. Reverend Adams. They were at Granny's yesterday and ate lunch with all of us."

"He seems like a nice fellow. I'm looking forward to hearing him preach this Sunday."

"He kind of makes me nervous."

"Why?"

"He kept staring at me all through lunch."

"Does he know you?"

"I don't know him. I can't think of why he would know me."

"Well, they're visiting here tonight. Better get in there."

He reached to open the door. "You be careful out there tonight, Mr. Pete."

"I will, son. Good night, now. See you in the morning."

Ma invited the preachers in, but Hank stayed in the yard, gazing at the stars overhead before going in himself. *God, please keep him safe tonight. Keep them all safe. Help them find that cat so we can get back to normal around here.* He took a couple of steps. *I can't believe I just said that. This has been the most exciting summer of my life, and I want things back to normal.* He stepped through the door.

"Here he is, reverend. Hank, Reverend Adams is here to see you, son."

He swallowed past the lump stuck in his throat. "Me?"

CHAPTER 16

Hank looked back outside in time to see the deputy's red car lights disappear into the night as he turned onto the road and moved toward town.

"Hank, where are your manners, son?"

"That's all right, Mrs. Baker. I'd be nervous if a stranger wanted to talk with me, too. Don't worry, son. It won't take long. I felt a connection to you yesterday and have felt compelled to seek you out to deliver a message from the Lord."

"Hank, why don't you and Reverend Adams talk on the porch. It will be more private. I'll keep your supper warm, son. Dr. Warden, Pastor Bob, would you like some peach cobbler? It's freshly made today. I'll keep some aside for you two when you're all done talking."

"Don't be too long, Calvin. Dr. Warden and I know very well about Mrs. Baker's peach cobbler. You'll think you've died and gone to heaven." Pastor Bob stood and rubbed his hands together. "Lead the way, Mrs. Baker. The good doctor and I are right behind you."

"Shall we go to the porch then, Hank?" The circuit preacher held the screen door open for him.

"Sure."

They sat on the top step; the preacher looked into the sky. "I love the summer nights here. You can see so many more stars than in the big city. Look how deep they go."

Hank looked from the sky to the reverend. He rubbed his hands together in slow motion. "It's my favorite thing to do at night, watch the stars. They make me dizzy if I stand and look directly overhead."

The preacher chuckled. "They are beautiful." He looked around the yard and pointed at the fireflies dancing in the air at the edge of the woods near the trail to the fishing hole. "I miss that, too, when I'm in the city."

"Reverend, what was it you wanted to talk with me about exactly?" Hank then remembered the questions he had asked God. *Okay, God. I have some questions for you. If you're really out there, you'll answer them. Granny's in trouble because of Sadie. Mr. Pete's in trouble according to Granny, but I don't know how or why. Mr. Morgan's in trouble because of the bounty. Will you make these troubles go away and keep my friends safe? I know Mr. Pete is a good man...So what's keeping me from saying he should ask Ma to marry him? There's really no reason for Ma not to get married again, is there? So why does her marrying him bother me so much?*

"You want some answers from God. When I saw you yesterday, I knew you were the one God had told me about."

"God told you about me, about my questions? I don't understand."

"Before I preach a revival, I spend a lot of time in prayer about what to preach and how to minister to the people who will attend. Whenever I pray about this revival, I'm burdened about a boy who is concerned about his family and friends. When I asked God specifically about how to minister to this boy, he reminded me of an incident in my past that still bothers me today. I think it might somehow be related to your needs. You see, I have been where you are."

"You know what I'm struggling with?"

"Let me explain it like this. When I was about your age…you're what? Twelve, thirteen?"

"Twelve."

The preacher bowed his head and nodded. "Yep. I was your age when my father died. He had been sick and developed a fever that eventually killed him. Now, mind you, I was angry and very distressed. Years later, I think it was seven or eight, my mother met a gentleman who fell in love with her and she fell in love with him. He wanted to marry her; but I made their lives so difficult, accusing them of terrible things. I took the anger I had for my dad dying out on *her*. I felt she was being unfaithful to my father, which wasn't true because he was gone. She had fulfilled her marriage vows with him when death parted them. But I selfishly made her feel so guilty that she refused to marry her gentleman. He left us alone, and she never considered marriage again as long as she lived. Now she was a young woman when my father died, and she lived to be almost ninety years old. She wasn't bitter or angry with me, but she was very lonely. I had selfishly taken her chance at true happiness away from her. It was like she died that day her gentleman friend left us. She never knew I heard her cry herself to sleep more often than I care to count." He took out a handkerchief and blew his nose, folding it up again to return to his coat pocket.

Hank stared at his hands, remembering. *I realize with everything going on and all, it may not be the best time to ask. I've been thinking about this for a while, now. If you haven't noticed, I've…I've fallen in love with your ma, Hank. I want to ask her to marry me.*

The preacher's voice broke. "I never asked her to forgive me, and she died with that unfinished business on my conscience for nearly fifty years now. I don't know why God led me to you with this, but I know there's a reason. If you are struggling with a situation similar to this, I urge you to not make the same mistake I made. My mother deserved the happiness I took away from her. She never complained, but she was always sad. She tried to hide it, but her eyes always gave her away."

"Do you still miss your father?"

"Oh, yes. You never stop missing your loved ones who die, but the pain I caused my mother is far worse than the grief I have experienced for either of them. Sometimes God gives us another person to love and care for us when a special loved one dies. I shudder to think of what I've missed because I wouldn't let him put that gentleman in my life."

"Do you mind if I ask you a question?"

"Go ahead. I won't promise I'll have an answer, but I'll try."

"Why does God let bad stuff happen? Pastor Bob says God can do anything. Why doesn't he stop the bad stuff?"

"Believe it or not, that's a good question, young man. It doesn't have an easy answer, though." He stopped rubbing his hands together and looked directly into Hank's eyes.

"I'm listening."

"I believe you are." He smiled and looked back at the stars. "You see, son, God is a gentleman. When someone makes a decision, he honors it. When Adam chose to eat from the forbidden tree, God kept his promise that death would come. Now when you think about it, Adam didn't just cause man to die, but all of creation. You see, in order for death to happen, bad things are going to happen. It's a law of nature since the fall of man. It wasn't God's plan, but it was Adam's choice. Is it fair? Not really, but we are products of that original sin. Think of it this way. The good doctor in there can tell you there are some diseases that are hereditary. Do you know what that means?"

"Yes, sir."

"Okay, then you know a hereditary disease means if you have it, someone in your family history had it, too. Right?"

"Yes, sir."

"That's what Adam did for us. He passed down his disease of sin because he chose free will over obedience. God kept his promise to punish that sin because that's who he is. If he didn't keep that one promise, we couldn't trust him, not really. Is it fair that a little baby have the hereditary disease his great-great-great grandfather had? Maybe not, but that's not the point. His relation to that great-great-great grandfather made him vulnerable to it. Because we all have Adam in our ancestry, we all have the problem with sin he gave us through the events that took him out of the Garden of Eden. We have inherited it through our blood relation to Adam. None of us are exempt from that problem. Every man who has lived was born with sin because of our relationship with Adam. The good news is what God did to make sure we didn't have to live with sin forever. He sent Jesus to die on the cross to pay the penalty of death for that sin once and for all. God gives us a chance to cure the sin problem eternally. But as long as we're in these human bodies, we're going to be subject to the consequences of our being related to Adam."

Hank nodded.

"I know that was a long way around to the answer of your question. But I want to be sure I answered your question. And more importantly, did God use me to answer your questions to your satisfaction?"

Wow, God, you really are out there, aren't you?

"Yes, sir, you did. But there's still one more."

"He must be going to answer that one later because I'm all done with what he sent me to do." The preacher grinned. "How about some peach cobbler?"

"Sure." Hank offered to shake the reverend's hand. "Thank you. I think I know what I need to do now."

Reverend Adams shook his hand. "Good man. You still working over at Mrs. Massey's farm? I mean, Granny's farm tomorrow?"

"Yes, sir."

"Well, then, we'd best get in there to that cobbler so you can rest up."

"Yes, sir, I'll have some right after I eat supper."

"Let me know if I can help with anything else."

"I will."

* * * * * * *

As Hank lay in bed later, he thought about all the circuit preacher had said. *God, I guess I can give Mr. Pete my answer now; but I have one more question you haven't answered yet. If Granny's right, Mr. Pete is still in trouble. I still don't know what kind of trouble, but she's real worried about him. So am I. Please keep him safe from the cat and any other kind of trouble there is out there. I need you to do this for me. I don't want to lose another father, please.*

When he opened his eyes, he caught a glimpse of Jimmy climbing into bed. "Where have you been? We're not supposed to go to the outhouse after dark, not until the cat's taken care of." He sat up on his elbow to see his brother better.

"I know. I wasn't in the outhouse."

"Then where have you been?" Frustration seeped into his voice.

"Nowhere. Just go back to sleep."

"Jimmy…"

"Look, I was checking under my bed, okay? I thought I heard something and needed to check it out. I didn't want Ma to scream if it was a mouse. You know how she is about them. Now, leave me alone. I'm sleepy."

Hank watched his brother turn his back to him. He shook his head, getting out of bed. He tiptoed to the other bed and leaned over Jimmy, seeing his eyes shut. He watched his breathing, amazed that it was already even with sound sleep. *What's he up to?*

When Hank looked under the bed, he saw what looked like a white pillow. He pulled it out, but it wasn't a pillow. It was one of Ma's petticoats. *What?* He looked again under the bed, but nothing else was there. He was perplexed at the petticoat then looked at Jimmy. *What is this?* He stuffed the garment back under the bed and returned to his own side of the room. *He must have been sleepwalking again.* Even with the heat and night critters, it didn't take long to go back to sleep.

The next time he opened his eyes, it was morning. The rooster crowed from the chicken yard; and the songbirds were chattering away. Hank yawned, looking across the room at his sleeping brother, and shook his head at the petticoat under the bed. *That's the strangest thing he's done up till now.*

Stepping across the room, he shook Jimmy. "Hey, it's morning. Are you going to help with the chores today?"

His little brother swatted at his hand. "Nobody can climb as fast as I can. Just close your eyes and count to ten."

"Hey, Jimmy! Wake up. It's morning."

He sat up and scratched his head. His hair stuck up and out all over his head.

"You awake? It's time to get up to do the chores."

Jimmy yawned and got up.

"Why do you have one of Ma's petticoats under your bed? Does she know it's missing?"

His little brother froze, then moved in slow motion, making his bed. "Uh, there's a petticoat under my bed?"

"Yeah. And what were you muttering about climbing faster than anyone else?"

He faced Hank, his face pale. Then he smoothed out a wrinkle in his top sheet. "I said that? Uh, just dreaming, I guess. I need to get dressed now so we can do chores."

Hank wasn't angry, but he couldn't let his brother think so. Instead, he was laughing to himself. *Golden Eagle, huh?* "You're strange, you know that? You'd better be careful, or someone's liable to send you to Benton."

"What's in Benton?"

"The insane asylum."

161

Jimmy's eyes widened. Hank chuckled and ruffled his unruly hair. "Don't worry. Ma won't let them take you away. She'd miss you too much. Hurry up and get dressed."

* * * * * * *

After breakfast, Mr. Pete drove the kids to Granny's. Hank was impressed with how awake he looked, even though he'd been on duty part of the night. When they arrived at her house, Granny met them in the front yard. The lines on her forehead caused Hank's heart to skip a beat. "Have any of you seen Jeffrey?"

Hank looked from her to the other kids to Mr. Pete. "If he was with the sheriff's men yesterday, maybe he stayed up all night watching for the cat."

Pete's brows came together in deep furrows. "He wasn't with us yesterday. I thought he was here."

Granny shook her head and looked in the direction of the woods behind her property. "He had promised to be here early to help the boys today, but he hasn't shown up. That's not like him."

Daniel shaded his eyes against the morning sun. "Maybe he had business in town."

Granny shook her head again. "No, he said he was finished traveling until next month. Besides, he doesn't go off without telling me, at least."

Pete cocked his head. "Why you?"

Granny's face turned a shade redder than it had been. "He knows I'll worry if I don't see him...I guess."

"Okay, I guess that makes sense. I need to get to the office to check in. I'll see if Stan has seen or heard from him. If he hasn't, I'll see if we can spare some men to try to find him."

Hank's neck began to tingle. "You don't think he's hurt, do you?"

"No, son. He's around somewhere. You know how he likes to be alone. I'll see you later. We'll find him."

The kids watched Granny and Mr. Pete walk toward his motor car.

"I'm getting that feeling again, guys."

Beth Ann looked at Hank. "You think he's in trouble?"

He paused, looking at the woods behind where the dog pen had been. "Yeah, I do."

CHAPTER 17

HANK STOPPED DIGGING TO WIPE his face with his handkerchief. He estimated his hole for an outhouse for the tent meetings was a little more than two feet deep. Abraham and Daniel were about ten feet away on either side of him, digging two more holes. From his best guess, they appeared to be about as far along in their work as he was.

Hank watched Daniel climb out of his hole. "Hey, what are you doing. It has to be at least six feet deep before we're finished, remember?"

He pointed toward the house. "Look. Isn't that the deputy? And look how many others are with him."

The other two looked toward the house. Hank's heart skipped a beat. "I knew it. Mr. Morgan's in trouble."

The boys abandoned their shovels and left the holes to join the search for their giant friend.

Hank forced himself not to run. *Please, God, let him be okay.* He pointed with his chin. "Isn't that Cliff with the deputy?" They all picked up speed.

When they arrived at the crowd surrounding the deputy, he was using a map to chart assignments to smaller groups.

Daniel put his hands on his hips and looked at the faces. "Wow! He's going to be surprised at how many people are here."

Hank made eye contact with Mr. Pete. The furrowed brows on the deputy worried him, but the slight nod of Deputy Collins' chin kept him from panicking. *At least he doesn't look annoyed with me.* He noticed several of the men had rifles or shotguns. *Please don't let them shoot Mr. Morgan by accident.*

"Are you sure Mr. Morgan's missing and not just hiding out?" Cliff's words caused hot anger to flush Hank's cheeks. His fingernails dug into his palms as he strained to control his white-knuckled fists before he faced him.

Daniel forced his way between them. His nose almost touched Hank's. "Don't let him push you into a fight. You'll lose. Believe me, I know. It's his favorite trick, but you'll be the one in trouble—not him." He turned toward his cousin. "Why do you have to be so mean? You're nothing but a bully. I'm done with you, and I'm tired of you treating my friends like they don't matter. You talk so big, but you're nothing but a coward trying to be something you're not. If you want respect, you have to earn it. As far as I'm concerned you don't have it in you. You judge people without getting to know them first. Then it doesn't matter how much they prove themselves, you still disrespect them. You obviously don't respect yourself or you'd be able to see the good in the people who deserve it. I wish you'd go home."

Cliff's nostrils flared. "Maybe you're just too gullible for your own good. And I can't wait to go home. At least then I can be myself without you harping on everything I do."

Hank took a couple of breaths, then he took a step backwards. He kept his fists tight at his sides. "If you don't believe Mr. Morgan's in trouble, why are you here?"

Cliff sidestepped Daniel. "It's the chance to see just who this guy really is. You guys live in a fantasy world. You wouldn't know danger if it came up and introduced itself to you." He took a couple of breaths, his eyes never leaving Hank's. "I tell you what. When we find him and if he's who you say he is, I'll apologize. But if he's not, you'll apologize to me. What do you say?"

Hank took a few seconds to think about his offer. Then he offered a handshake. "All right, deal. Shake on it?"

Cliff looked at the hand offered him without making a move.

Hank taunted his challenger. "Are you scared you'll be wrong?"

After another few seconds, they shook hands without saying another word. Then Cliff returned to the groups waiting for their assignments.

"Come on, guys, let's get our search assignments from Mr. Pete." He looked at the faces milling around. "Hey, where's Abraham?"

Daniel put his hands in his pockets. "I don't know. I was sort of busy. I can't believe I stood up to him. My knees are still shaking."

"You did good, Daniel." Hank put a hand on his shoulder. "Enough about Cliff. We have more important things to do." He craned to see the people moving toward the woods. "Oh, well. Abraham knows where we are. Besides, we make a pretty good team by ourselves, just the two of us."

"Except maybe Beth Ann."

Hank smiled. "Yeah, but not this time. Come on, partner."

There were two other teams ahead of them. When it was their turn, Pete rolled up the map.

"What about us, Mr. Pete. We want to help."

"I appreciate your willingness, Hank; but I can't let you do that. I'd rather you be here when the teams check in. I don't want you in the woods as long as that cat is out there."

"But Cliff..." His pulse pounded in his ears.

"He's with his dad and another man. I can't let you and Daniel go alone. That would be irresponsible of me, to say nothing about what your folks would say or do to me for letting you go. Sorry."

"But..." Tears burned his eyes.

"Hank, no! Now you promised you wouldn't put yourself in danger in those woods, remember? Well, that has to be my promise, too. I will not put you intentionally in danger in those woods or anywhere else. These other teams have weapons in case they come upon the cat or a rabies-infected animal. They're prepared and properly equipped. You aren't. Now, please, I have a job to do. Don't let me down, son."

Daniel came up beside him as Hank watched the deputy go inside the house.

"What do we do now?"

"I don't know, but…"

Beth Ann joined them in the yard. "Granny's so worried. She's afraid something's happened to Mr. Morgan, especially with those bounty posters still up."

Hank put his hands in his pockets. "I am, too."

Daniel looked toward the woods beyond the backyard. "Is Abraham in the house?"

"No. Why?"

"He was here with us, then he wasn't. I thought maybe he went inside."

Hank kicked up a small dirt cloud. "He's around somewhere. You know, we've been a team all summer. There's no sense in wasting our talents now. The three of us need to do what we do best. Well, at least there's something *you* can do, Beth Ann. Keep your ears open; and let us know if you hear anything important, no matter where it comes from. In the meantime, Daniel and I should get back to the digging since Mr. Pete won't let us help with the search." He pointed out where they'd be. "We'll be just over that hill digging the outhouse holes."

"You can depend on me. Be careful out there." Beth Ann turned to go inside; Hank and Daniel set out for the unfinished job in the open field.

* * * * * * *

Nearly an hour after returning to work, Hank was so focused on the digging, he jumped when Beth Ann asked if he and Daniel were thirsty for some fresh lemonade. They climbed out of their respective holes and removed their gloves. Hank drained his glass in one long drink.

Daniel smacked his lips. "That was good." As he gave his glass back to Beth Ann, he belched, sounding like a bullfrog, causing them all to double over with gut-wrenching laughter.

When they regained control, Beth Ann wiped her eyes. "I haven't laughed that hard in a long time. Thank you, Daniel, even though your manners are less than desirable sometimes."

"Sorry. Excuse me. It just came out. Besides, what good is it if you can't be yourself around your best friends?"

Hank wiped tears from his eyes. "Don't worry. You did us a service the way only you can. I've been so tense; I haven't been able to laugh, really laugh. But I couldn't stop just now. I feel better—I think."

Beth Ann frowned, looking between the boys and behind them. She pointed with her chin. "Is that Abraham?"

The boys turned in the direction she pointed. Abraham was running toward them. He almost stumbled once, but kept upright, racing across the field.

Hank's pulse quickened. "Where's he been?"

He slowed to a fast walk the last several yards, his mouth open and his hand spread over his heart. When he reached them, he could barely talk. "I need your help...Mr. Morgan...he's out there." He pointed back to where he'd come through the woods. "He's hurt...real bad."

Hank's knees almost buckled. "Where? What happened? How'd you find him?"

"I'll explain later. We need to get to him, get him back here so Granny and Beth Ann can do their doctor thing on him. He's lost a lot of blood already."

"But he's so big. How are we going to get him back here?" Daniel was talking to himself, but Hank had asked himself the same question.

Beth Ann switched into doctor mode with the voice of authority. "Make a *travois*."

Daniel scrunched his brows together. "A what? Oh, wait, you mean like what the Indians used to carry sick or injured people on? A stretcher-like thing you hook up to a horse or mule?"

"Yeah. Hank, get one of the mules. Abraham needs to get his wind. And grab a sheet off the clothesline, too."

Hank understood Beth Ann's plan and acted on her suggestions without questions. Right now, he didn't care about his promise to Mr. Pete to stay out of the woods. *This is more important. I won't let Mr. Morgan die. If Mr. Pete is at the house, I'll tell him so he can help. If he isn't, I'm going to do what has to be done. If I get in trouble, then I get in trouble.* He went immediately to the barn to harness whichever mule was closest. When the harness was in place, Hank climbed on Samson's back, reaching for a sheet as he passed the clothesline. With the wadded sheet in hand, he kicked the mule into a gallop, riding back to the others as fast as he dared, dismounting when he arrived.

Daniel took the reins Hank tossed. "What about what the deputy told you, Hank?"

"He wasn't at the house. We can't wait on him. Mr. Morgan needs us now."

"What if we see the cat?"

Hank looked around. "Grab the shovels. We'll use them as weapons if we need them." With their shovels in hand and Samson in tow, Abraham led the way through the woods.

* * * * * * *

"How much further?" Hank's fears grew with every anxious step.

"We're almost there."

"How did you know where he would be?"

"He told me so if Granny ever needed him I'd know where to find him. He made me swear to keep it a secret. He really

likes his solitude. I didn't see a problem not telling anyone…
till today, anyway. We're here." Abraham ran to the giant lying
prone near his camp.

Hank scanned the treetops and around the camp. He almost
missed the tent that was well camouflaged, except for the
opening. "Here, Daniel, let's make the *travois*. Abraham, make
sure he's still breathing."

"What are we going to use for poles?"

"If we can't find anything, we'll have to use the shovels."

Abraham breathed heavily. "He's barely breathing, but he's
still alive."

Daniel put his hands on his hips. "If we were closer to the
river, we might could find some felled trees, but there aren't any
around here. I guess we'll have to use the shovels."

Hank shook the sheet out then folded it once, forming a double
layer for the bed of the *travois*. "They'll have to do. Let's tie the
corners to them then tie the reins to the handles to pull him to
Granny's. Make sure the shovel parts are closer together to keep
from dragging Mr. Morgan on the ground with just the sheet under
him. That might help get him to the house quicker, too."

They worked quickly and quietly, talking only to guide
each other's progress. Sweat poured from Hank's hairline and
underarms as they struggled to get the giant on the *travois*,
careful not to do further damage to the cuts on his legs. After
what seemed like hours, they were on their way to Granny's.
Daniel rode Samson while Hank and Abraham guided him
from either side of the harness. As they made their way through
the woods, Hank realized the only sounds he heard were from
Samson's heavy hooves and the *travois* being dragged.

"Wait, stop." It was eerily quiet. The hair on the back of Hank's
neck bristled and the tingle returned. "You hear that?"

Abraham looked at him from around Samson's snout. "You
mean other than the quiet?"

A low growl echoed across the treetops, making it impossible to know exactly where it came from. "That!"

Samson snorted and pranced. Hank noticed his haunches twitch. "Whoa, boy! Don't let him bolt, please." Daniel shifted on the mule's back. "Uh, we only have one shovel, guys."

The cat was definitely getting closer; but it wasn't on the ground if Hank had judged the growls correctly. "I think it smells the blood." His body trembled, and his mouth was completely dry. Without spit, it was hard to swallow. "Let's just keep moving… slowly." He and Abraham pulled Samson, but the mule resisted until another growl sounded closer still.

Hank's heart stopped when he heard the snap of a twig just ahead. He nearly fainted when a shot rang out, the bullet whizzing close overhead. A heavy thud behind them made the mule buck slightly, nearly unseating Daniel. Wide-eyed, Hank turned, seeing a large lump of black fur on the path just a few feet away. His head jerked forward as Deputy Collins lowered his rifle, a scowl relaxing between his brows.

The edges of Hank's peripheral vision blackened as he felt the blood drain from his face. His legs folded under him, but he stayed conscious…barely. He lowered his head to get the blood back to his face. His head itched all over.

"You boys all right?"

Hank heard his friends respond, but he could only move his mouth.

The deputy knelt beside the *travois*, setting the rifle on the ground and testing the sturdiness of the knots. "How's Mr. Morgan?"

Abraham patted Samson's neck and muzzle. "He's bad, sir."

"Let's get him to Granny's. She and Beth Ann are waiting for him.

* * * * * * *

It was early evening when Mr. Pete joined Hank on the top step of

Granny's front porch. Hank held his head between his hands, his elbows anchored on his knees. He didn't know how much time had passed waiting for word about Mr. Morgan's condition.

"How is he?"

The deputy rested his arms over his knees. "He's going to be laid up for a while, but he'll mend. The cuts weren't too deep. The good news is the bleeding cleansed the wounds for the most part."

"Was it the cat?" He peeked at Mr. Pete, who was looking across the yard.

"No, he keeps mumbling about a monster razorback—his words, not mine; but he has a fever. It will be a day or so before we hear his story."

"He's not infected with rabies, is he?"

"I don't think so. His injuries don't match the animals we've had reported being infected."

"But Buster was cut up, too."

"Whatever he got into a fight with was along the size of a bobcat or big coon. The injuries to Mr. Morgan are from something much larger. I guess it could have been from a razorback, but we won't know for sure till he wakes up." It was silent between them for almost a minute.

Hank felt the deputy's stare. *May as well get this over with. Stop stalling. Time to take responsibility for my actions.* Hank raised his head and squared his shoulders; and then he looked directly at him, unwavering. The butterflies in his stomach felt like bats. "I know you're probably angry with me for breaking my promise; but if we hadn't gone, I believe Mr. Morgan would be dead. I didn't just go without thinking through my options. When I came up to the house to get Samson, I looked for you to tell you; but you weren't here. I had decided if I couldn't find you, I'd have to do what I did, no matter what punishment I had to take. It was a matter of life or death. I chose to save a life."

Mr. Pete wrapped an arm around Hank's shoulders. "I know. You did good, son. I am especially proud of how you handled yourself when I found you and saw the cat in the trees behind you. You did everything right. But…"

"I know. I still broke a promise and have to deal with the consequences of my actions."

The deputy smiled. "Your daddy taught you well."

Hank wiped his palms on his trousers. "Does Ma have to know? About today, I mean." Mr. Pete raised one eyebrow and lowered his head, his eyes telling Hank what he was dreading. "Yeah, I thought so." In spite of the weight on his shoulders, his stomach rumbled. "Oh, yeah. I've been meaning to ask you, are you and Mr. Morgan cousins?"

The deputy stopped rubbing his hands together and looked at Hank with furrowed brows. "No, I don't think so. What makes you think we're cousins?"

"Something I heard him tell Granny. I must have misunderstood."

"Eavesdropping again?"

"Not exactly."

Mr. Pete stood, hooking his thumbs on either side of his belt buckle. "Well, everyone has gone home except you, Dr. Warden, and Beth Ann. The sun will be down in another half-hour. I should get you home. Did I see you and Cliff shaking hands earlier?"

Hank stood, too, stretching his legs. "Yeah. He apologized for being an idiot about Mr. Morgan, except he didn't call himself an idiot. But he *did* finally admit he was wrong about him."

The deputy nodded while his eyebrows moved up then back down. "That was mighty big of him."

"He's all right, I guess. But I have to say a little of him goes a long way, especially for Daniel."

The deputy chuckled. "I could see that."

"Can I ask you a question?"

"Sure."

"Do you know a long way home?"

Mr. Pete chuckled again. "I'm afraid not. Enough stalling. Let's go."

"Okay." When they reached the motor car, Hank remembered his conversation with the circuit preacher. He waited till they were seated inside the car. "Oh yeah. I almost forgot."

The deputy waited to start the engine. "What?"

"You still want to ask Ma to marry you? Before you answer, you'd better think about what you're getting into if she says yes. I'm not promising I won't mess up. But I will always have a good reason for doing what I do."

Mr. Pete's grin lit his whole face. "You're okay with us getting married if she says yes?"

"Yes, sir."

www.ingramcontent.com/pod-product-compliance
Lightning Source LLC
Chambersburg PA
CBHW020642180626
46816CB00003B/1089